Guy turned to her as
whom he was talking to
kid. You take care of yo

"You're not leaving—you can't leave!" she said, fighting against the tears. "Beth doesn't matter. Forget her! You still have your art." *And you have me,* she added silently.

"I think we both know art isn't everything, Nessa. It isn't enough for me, and I know you want more. You don't need me to help you follow your dreams. You can do it—but guard your heart. Someday, when you're all grown up, you'll find someone special and worthy of your love." He gave her a final hug, gripping her tight, before he released her.

Janessa stood in shocked silence as he slowly walked away without a backward glance. As he closed the door her tears began to fall. "I don't have to wait for someday. I've already found the person I love."

**TISH DAVIS** lives in Florida with her husband and three sons. When she isn't homeschooling, she is busy writing inspirational romance. *To the Extreme* was her first published novel. Tish hopes her writing will entertain, uplift, and draw her readers into a closer relationship with the Lord.

Books by Tish Davis

**HEARTSONG PRESENTS**
HP426—To the Extreme
HP477—Extreme Grace
HP557—If You Please
HP638—Real Treasure
HP694—Riches of the Heart

# Safe in His Arms

*Tish Davis*

Heartsong Presents

To Bradley, my best friend and love of my life. You're the best.

A note from the Author:
*I love to hear from my readers! You may correspond with me by writing:*

**Tish Davis**
**Author Relations**
**PO Box 721**
**Uhrichsville, OH 44683**

**ISBN 978-1-59310-973-8**

**SAFE IN HIS ARMS**

*Our mission is to publish and distribute inspirational products offering exceptional value and biblical encouragement to the masses.*

PRINTED IN THE U.S.A.

# *prologue*

"Do I love you? Of course not! How could I love someone who doesn't understand my needs?"

Janessa flinched at the abrasive words and covered her mouth to hold back her cry of protest. Her heart ached—not for herself but for the man who received the rejection. If she could, she'd jump out and defend him. But then they would know she'd been hiding in the supply closet, listening to every word.

"How can you do this to me, Beth? You're leaving because I won't pay for your plastic surgery? What kind of reason is that?"

"You should know a model has to do everything in her power to stay beautiful. I earn my living with my looks—by being so beautiful that everyone wants the clothes I wear, the makeup I use, the suntan oil I put on, every sports car I model. It's a tough business, and if you won't help me stay perfect, I'll find someone who will."

Janessa wanted to jump out and scream that Beth was a fraud. She'd done everything she could to separate Guy from the people who loved him because she was jealous. She wanted him to herself—as long as he was giving her enough money. And with the money he made from his paintings he could afford to give Beth anything she desired. Why didn't he see he was being used? Beth was only interested in him for what he could provide. But Janessa loved him for himself.

"I could have chosen any model to work for me, but I chose

you. I know your face better than the lines of my own reflection. Don't do this to me."

"You did it to yourself," Beth retorted.

Janessa peeked out of the closet as Beth turned on her heel and stormed out of the room. "Guy?" she called softly, no longer caring that she had been eavesdropping.

He was slouched on a stool, staring unseeing out the window. His latest painting of Beth stood on the easel beside him. The canvas had been torn.

Slowly she approached him. She longed to put her arms around him and comfort him as he always comforted her when she was upset. "She doesn't matter. I told you she wasn't right for you. She went to church with us, but she didn't believe. She pretended to like me, but she was mean whenever you left the room. Even Walter doesn't like her."

"Yeah," he responded with a forced laugh that sounded more like a groan. "I suppose you were listening."

She nodded grimly, too concerned to feel ashamed.

"What's Walter going to say about this work of art? He won't be too impressed with his protégé." She motioned to the ruined canvas.

"That doesn't matter either!" When she put her hand on his shoulder he shrugged it off.

"Nothing matters anymore. I need to get out of here."

"What do you mean? Where are you going?" Janessa asked, feeling a panic rise within her. She'd never seen him this upset.

Guy turned to her as though he'd just realized whom he was talking to. "Don't worry about me, kid. You take care of yourself."

"You're not leaving—you can't leave!" she said, fighting against the tears. "Beth doesn't matter. Forget her! You still have your art." *And you have me,* she added silently.

"I think we both know art isn't everything, Nessa. It isn't enough for me, and I know you want more. You don't need me to help you follow your dreams. You can do it—but guard your heart. Someday, when you're all grown up, you'll find someone special and worthy of your love." He gave her a final hug, gripping her tight, before he released her.

Janessa stood in shocked silence as he slowly walked away without a backward glance. As he closed the door her tears began to fall. "I don't have to wait for someday. I've already found the person I love."

## one

"Something's about to happen. I can't explain how I know. . . it's just a feeling I have deep inside, and it won't go away. You have to help—you're the only one I trust," Walter pleaded.

Guy jerked the phone away from his ear and stared at it incredulously, thinking he must be dreaming. He'd never heard Walter Richards, world-renowned artist, ask anyone for help.

"Tell me what you need," he responded, praying it was within his power. Walter was a demanding taskmaster, often expecting more than was humanly possible for most people, but Guy had always done his best to achieve the impossible for Walter. The man had been like a father after all.

"My granddaughter, Janessa, is in the middle of something—something sinister—and she's too inexperienced and trusting. In fact, I think she's too shortsighted to see past the end of her nose to what's really going on. I need you to protect her, Guy. Find a way to get close to her and keep her safe. I'd do it myself, but she would never let me near. Protect her. Please. I'll make it worth your while."

"Isn't this a job for the police or even a bodyguard?"

"I've talked to the Rochester Police Department, but without anything concrete to go on they don't have the time to 'entertain my whims,' so they told me. And as for a bodyguard, that's what you'll be. Janessa would never tolerate a strange man following her around, but she knows you."

Guy wasn't so sure. "Why me? We haven't seen each other

for ten years, so I'm no different from a stranger to her. And if she's in danger, don't you want someone more qualified? The best I can offer is a few karate moves from lessons when I was a kid."

Walter wasn't to be swayed. "There's no one else I can trust. And she needs you whether she realizes it or not. Get a job at the museum. I want you working alongside her. And I'm not asking you to take up painting again," he hurried on as though sensing Guy's reluctance. "It's your choice to waste your talent, and I won't badger you about that anymore. Right now I'm asking you to help my granddaughter. Keep her out of trouble."

"What trouble?"

"I can't say exactly! I just know in my heart she needs your help. Will you do it?"

Silence stretched on the line as Guy considered what Walter's request might entail. Working in the museum put a different twist on the job, and he was tempted to refuse. He'd put a wide distance between himself and anything artistic, and it would be the first time in ten years he'd set foot in a museum. The notion made him bristle with discomfort. Yet he'd prayed that God would fix the ache that never left his heart. Perhaps he would find the healing he searched for if he went in this direction.

"Yes, Walter, I'll do it. I'll do my very best to protect your granddaughter."

&

Janessa stared in disbelief at the man standing in the doorway of her workroom. He was here—now? She hadn't seen Guy Langly for many years, but she would have recognized him anywhere. His image was permanently etched in her mind since she'd foolishly fallen in love with him as a teenager. As he stood there staring at her with blue eyes and unsmiling lips she again felt like the gauche young girl who'd followed him around for two years so long ago. Her brownish blond hair was pulled back in a haphazard ponytail, similar to how she wore it as a teen. When she took care to brush it to a sheen, her hair could look like a wave of dark wheat flowing just past her shoulders. Today it looked scraggly and untidy as she pushed the tendrils away while she worked. She wasn't wearing contacts, and thick lenses masked her hazel eyes. Glasses always seemed easier to deal with in the morning. And her clothes were oversized and splattered with paint even though she wore a smock—a garbage bag would look better. Janessa stifled a groan, wishing she might sink through the floor. If only God would turn back the hands of time so she could start the day over!

Her friend and coworker, Rosy Moore, giggled nervously next to Janessa, making her feel all the more self-conscious.

"Hi, Nessa. It's been a long time," Guy said in his deep voice that made her heart flutter. He stepped into the room carrying a toolbox and not the art materials she associated with him. When he set the toolbox on her tottering desk and turned back to her, Janessa quickly hid her frown of confusion.

Rosy gave her a curious look, and Janessa knew her friend had a million questions about who Guy was. No one called her Nessa anymore.

Guy didn't seem to notice her discomfort. "Is there anything you need to have fixed? I now work for the museum as a handyman of sorts. I've also taken on janitorial duties so if anything needs cleaning—" His gaze dropped to the dirty, paint-splattered floor. Janessa knew her workroom required more effort than his paycheck warranted.

She stared at him mutely, unable to form an intelligible answer. He'd caught her off guard, and making small talk went beyond her present capabilities.

Rosy wasn't about to be put off by the awkward silence. "I think we're okay." She gave Guy a welcoming smile. "I'm Rosy Moore, by the way."

Guy rewarded Rosy's efforts at conversation with one of his devastating smiles. "Guy Langly. I'm sure you'll see plenty of me. Call if you need anything—a new light bulb or whatever." He turned his gaze back to Janessa. "I'll talk to you later, and we can get caught up. Maybe we could go out for coffee or something."

Janessa muttered something that sounded more like a gurgle trapped in her throat. But he didn't seem to notice as he gathered his tools and left the workroom.

As soon as he was gone Rosy turned on her. "What was that about? I've never seen you get flustered over a man before!"

Janessa sighed in exasperation. How could she explain that one look at Guy turned her inside out and made her heart beat as though she'd run a marathon? She doubted Rosy had ever felt that way. Most men chased her, and she didn't have time to pine over any of them. There were so many things Rosy couldn't understand because they were different.

Where Janessa felt she was plain, her best friend was flamboyant. Rosy should have been in movies, not tucked in the back rooms of a museum. Her long black hair—not her natural color—was piled high on her head and pinned in place with a red silk peony that matched her red fingernails. Her dress with its large colorful flowers was too outlandish for most people, but it looked right on her. And on her feet she wore black ballerina slippers. She jingled with every movement because of the silver bracelets on her wrists, tiny bells hanging from her ears and rows of silver necklaces draping down to her waist. Beside her Janessa felt as inspiring as a dried-out sponge.

Fashionable appearances were never her forte. What she lacked in style, she made up with hard work. If something needed to be done, she took care of it. And the pile of work awaiting her attention proved people valued her ability. She glanced at the mountain of canvases stacked against the wall, awaiting restoration. Dull, dusty oil paintings covered with decades of abuse or neglect came alive with color when she gave them her special attention. Rosy was competent, but she moved much slower than Janessa did. Few people could match her speed and level of perfection.

Painting something from her own imagination was something she couldn't do easily, and she found it a grueling task. She had no talent of her own to create masterpieces as her grandfather, Walter Richards, did on a regular basis. Yet she could duplicate anything already painted. She was amazingly adept at reproducing and restoring the works of any artistic master. Copying the works of others was no great feat in her grandfather's eyes, and it could be considered a questionable talent so she kept her skill to herself. She never wanted to be considered an art forger, and restoration was just as rewarding for her. Everyone thought she was a genius at bringing new life to old paintings. She held a position of respect in the museum, but few people knew her success stemmed from her ability to recreate just about any oil painting, making the forgery an identical copy of the original.

"You're going to meet with him later, aren't you? I'd love to have something to talk about with that man." Rosy sighed. "You've never said anything about him, Janessa, but by the look on your face I'd guess he's someone important. He seems familiar."

Rosy's prattle faded as Janessa frowned in concentration. Janessa wasn't about to remind her friend that Guy Langly had been a promising artist, studying under her grandfather. Guy was a private part of her past, and she wanted to keep those days locked away.

"He wasn't serious," she muttered. *God, please don't let him be serious!* she prayed silently. She didn't want to talk about the "good ol' days" because in her mind nothing about them was good. The struggles with her grandfather had been heartbreaking. He'd wanted her to develop into a famous artist, following in his very big footsteps. She knew in her heart that wasn't right for her. And after months of praying she confronted her grandfather and told him she was quitting his tutelage to study art history. She didn't have any desire to create her own works and found the effort stressful and frustrating. Instead she wanted to study the masters.

Her grandfather had been furious. She knew he wanted her to carry on the family tradition where her father had failed to do so. Her dad had chosen photography over painting, disappointing her grandfather. Walter had put all his hope into Janessa, and she chose to disappoint him, as well. He knew of her ability to copy others' works, and he believed she could develop that talent into her own style. Janessa didn't agree, and her mind was made up to take another path. Her parents supported her decision and knew she would be happy with the direction she chose, but her grandfather wouldn't listen. No matter how she tried to assuage his anger he refused to compromise. And in the end, when she left for college at the age of eighteen, her grandfather disowned her. He vowed he was wiping his hands clean of her if she chose any direction but his. It wasn't easy, but she struck out on her own by first studying art history at Syracuse University and then later training in Florence, Italy.

Now she had very little contact with her grandfather, and when they did meet the conversation was always stilted and uncomfortable. She knew he was still displeased with her, but she couldn't change that, short of a miracle from God.

*And I'm still hoping for a miracle—that he'll wake up and realize I didn't mess up my life after all.* But she knew it would take willingness on her grandfather's part, as well, to mend their relationship.

"I have a great idea," Rosy said with a mischievous gleam in her eyes. "Why don't you take Guy to the museum's fund-raising benefit tomorrow night? It would be a perfect time for you to get reacquainted. And then he'll see you looking a little more glamorous," she added with a look of distaste at Janessa's clothes. "You *are* wearing the black evening gown I helped pick out and not something hideous from the depths of your closet?"

Janessa wasn't offended by Rosy's disapproval of her clothing. They often joked over their differences, and she knew Rosy loved her regardless of how she dressed. She was the only one, besides Janessa's parents, who appreciated her for herself. Guy Langly had tolerated a lovesick teenager who dogged his every step, but she doubted he ever took her seriously. Why would he notice her now?

"He wouldn't care if I wore a garbage bag, Rosy. So why don't you just drop this nonsense so we can get back to work? I have a busy schedule—as usual," she added with a sigh.

Turning back to the pile of canvases, she picked up the first one and set it on her worktable.

"The only reason you're behind is because you won't say no

to Ted Devroe. He may be the museum curator, but he has no right to enslave you the way he does. You work too hard."

It was another of Rosy's complaints, and Janessa knew it came from concern. She never turned down projects, though they were piling around her at the rate of a heavy snowfall. Ted knew she was good at her job and had no problem taking advantage of her willingness to work hard. How could she suddenly stop doing everything that was asked of her? It was her job, and she loved her work.

"Look at the time! I won't finish this old Gothic piece today anyway. I hate the period, and I bet Ted gave me this one because he knows I hate it," Rosy grumbled.

Janessa peered over her friend's shoulder at the detailed painting of a cathedral. She thought it was beautiful, if dark. "I can finish it for you."

"Tempting offer but no, thanks! You already have too much work without taking on mine. Let's quit for lunch and grab a slice of pizza." Rosy slid off her stool and reached for her jacket. "My treat."

"I can't. Mrs. Pembroke wants her painting done, and I really should finish it before tomorrow. She's such a sweet lady."

"A sweet lady who would never want you to skip lunch just to clean up her old ugly painting."

"I want it finished for her before the benefit," Janessa murmured absently as she turned back to her worktable. She studied the canvas and made a mental list of what was needed and how long it would probably take.

"Speaking of the benefit again, since you won't go with Guy that leaves the field wide open for Ted. You won't let him push you into going with him, will you?"

Janessa was barely listening. "Ted?"

"Yeah, Ted, the curator—our boss. Ted, the man who keeps trying to date you. He picks at you even more than I do. But you know I'm just teasing with you when I pick. He's serious."

"Ted means well. After all, he is a deacon in his church. He expects everyone to dress nicely," Janessa murmured.

"That's ridiculous, and you know it, Janessa. Just promise me you won't go with him. We can go together."

"What a great idea!" Janessa looked up and grinned at Rosy.

"It's a date then! And since you won't think of your own needs—I'm sure your stomach is rumbling just like mine—I'll bring you back a slice of pepperoni."

Once Rosy left and the room was quiet again, Janessa went to work on Mrs. Pembroke's painting. The style was an imitation of early American, but the piece was ugly with bold yellow flowers poked in an ill-formed vase. The frame was roughly cut, and it was one of the dirtiest canvases she'd seen in a long time, though she didn't think the painting was very old—maybe twenty or thirty years by the style of frame used. Mrs. Pembroke, a tiny seventy-year-old woman with bluish gray hair, flowery caftans, and a frisky poodle had brought her latest discovery straight to Janessa after pulling it from her attic. She said the house had been in her family for many generations and it seemed no one had ever gone through the storage room. Mrs. Pembroke felt the ugly painting had a very special purpose.

Janessa agreed as she stared at the ugly flowers. A painting so hideous could have only one purpose. "It's supposed to keep the mice away!"

"Are you talking to me, Janessa?"

"What? Oh!" Janessa turned at the sound of the familiar deep voice, and as she did so her sleeve caught the rough frame of the ugly painting. Before the painting could topple to the floor, Guy Langly reached around Janessa and steadied both her and the canvas. "I didn't know you were behind me. How did you sneak in here?"

"Feeling nervous?" His blue eyes sparkled with amusement though his lips remained in a grim line as he stared down at her. His gaze moved slowly from her eyes then focused on her mouth.

Seconds seemed to stretch as they gazed at one another, and Janessa had the funny notion he wanted to kiss her. If only her foolish imagination would stop playing tricks on her!

She remembered when she had first spent time with Guy. Twelve years earlier, when she was sixteen and he was twenty-two, he became her grandfather's protégé. She loved watching him paint. He truly enjoyed his artwork, even when Walter offered more criticism than praise.

Guy became incredibly successful in a brief amount of time with beautiful women clamoring to become his models, but he always had a kind word for Janessa. During snatches of private conversation he offered words of encouragement and even prayed with her when she needed consoling. He saw the frustration she had with her grandfather. When she threatened to run away, Guy helped her find different ways to please Walter. Even if her painting didn't please him, Guy promised that her diligence would get her grandfather's attention.

Janessa shook her head, forcing the memories back to the past, and the small movement broke the silent connection between them.

"Here, let me help you. Don't jerk your arm, or it'll rip your sweater."

"Don't worry about it. I can get it," she protested, but he proceeded to help her as though she hadn't spoken. "I should have been more careful."

Even now as she watched his long strong fingers untangle her sleeve from the rough frame she realized her foolish heart still cared for him. She was glad he didn't know her thoughts. It would be embarrassing if he knew how much she still longed for his love and affection and how her pulse raced when he was near. Remaining outwardly indifferent was difficult.

Guy's dark brows drew together in a frown as he studied her. "Are you okay? Anything bothering you?" he asked once he'd freed her sleeve.

Aside from his touch and the fact that she couldn't disengage her tongue from the roof of her mouth, yes, she was okay. Janessa blinked at him, willing her heart rate to slow. Having Guy touching her arm didn't make her feel any more relaxed. Why had he reappeared after vanishing from her life for ten years? Why was he working as a custodian in the museum when his artwork rivaled anything on display? Was she bothered? Absolutely!

She was saved from answering him when Ted Devroe, the museum curator—or Picky Taskmaster, as Rosy called him—stepped into the workroom. "Janessa, I'd like to speak to you. Alone," he said with a frown in Guy's direction.

As far as museum curators went, Ted was nothing like the stereotypes. He was thirty-five with classic Italian looks and was always dressed in the height of fashion. He claimed no real love for art; yet he had a brilliant mind for business. Often Janessa tried to explain what she did during those tedious hours of restoring a painting, but he wasn't interested. He wanted to know dollar figures.

She rose with a shrug and followed him to the door. Once she was in the dimly lit hallway, he jerked the door to her workroom closed, making her wince at the sharp sound. She knew he was upset without having to look up at his glowering face.

"Why is he in there, Janessa?"

She gave him a puzzled look when he didn't mention anything about her work. "Who, Guy?"

"Yes, Guy Langly. I'm aware you already know each other since he studied with your grandfather. I read it on his application. And Walter put in a good word for him. I didn't have much choice but to hire him. Yet that doesn't explain why he's in your workroom. Is he interested in you?"

It didn't seem like a professional question, and Ted had a tendency to overstep the boundaries into personal territory. It was no secret he wanted a relationship with her; yet she always shied away from him. While he claimed to be a Christian, was handsome and a business whiz, she couldn't picture herself with him. He always seemed to disapprove of her, and his jealousy didn't sit right.

"Guy is not interested in me. He's the janitor. I'd imagine he's going to clean something," she said with a defiant lift to her chin.

"Is that why he had hold of your arm?"

Color filled Janessa's cheeks, and she let her gaze drop. "He was keeping me from making a clumsy wreck of Mrs. Pembroke's painting when my sleeve got caught."

Ted reached out and gripped her shoulders. When she tried to pull away his grip tightened.

"Don't do that," she demanded uncomfortably.

His eyes darkened. "You know I want us to be closer, Janessa."

She couldn't move with her back against the wall and Ted pinning her by the shoulders. "You're my boss. Dating is not a good idea."

"And what about Langly? You work with him, too. Will that keep you from dating him if he asks?"

Janessa refused to answer since he had ventured into the personal territory that she refused to discuss with anyone. She didn't have any illusions of Guy asking her on a date. He wouldn't—not that it was any of Ted's business.

"I don't know why you're being difficult, Janessa, but you can make it up to me. Allow me to take you to the benefit tomorrow night. It can be in a professional capacity, if you insist."

"I'm sorry. I already have plans to go with someone else," Janessa responded, glad for Rosy's suggestion they go together. She could still hear her friend's warning that Ted would try to manipulate her into going with him.

Ted's glower deepened as he stared down at her. "With whom? Langly?"

"No! I doubt he'll even be there. Now, if you'll excuse me, I should get back to work."

Still Ted refused to move when she tried to wriggle out of his grasp. "That's another thing I want to talk to you about. Your work. I have several key pieces that have just come in from a prominent collector here in Rochester. They're recent acquisitions and need restoration. He said he wants them completed quickly. I promised it would be no problem, of course."

Janessa swallowed the lump of frustration that grew with Ted's words. She couldn't handle any more work. As it was, she had enough to keep her busy for the next three months, and she couldn't remember when she'd taken time off except for Sunday morning when she went to church. She wanted to tell him the collector needed to take his pieces somewhere else if he wanted them done quickly, but by the set of Ted's rigid expression there was no way she could turn down the work. She couldn't understand why he insisted on giving her so much to do when others were just as capable if not as fast.

"I'll find a way to get them done," she answered with a sigh, praying God would loosen her schedule that was already bursting at the seams. She knew Rosy would help where she could, but her workload was heavy, as well. It would mean longer hours into the evenings in addition to the early mornings she was already working.

"I knew you would." Ted flashed a grin guaranteed to make most women weak in the knees, but it didn't have much effect on Janessa. As he stepped back allowing her to leave, his grin slipped again into a serious expression. "Just keep Langly out of your workroom. I don't trust him."

# two

Ted's words replayed through Janessa's mind as she prepared Mrs. Pembroke's canvas for restoration. Why did he hire Guy if he didn't trust him? He said her grandfather had put in a good word for Guy, which probably meant he pressured Ted into hiring him. But why would Guy want to be a janitor and ignore his incredible artistic talent? And why would her grandfather want him working at *her* museum?

All these questions bubbled around in her mind, multiplying as she looked for reasonable answers. She would have asked Guy, but he'd slipped away soon after Ted's appearance, mumbling something about his own work. If Guy wanted to get back into the world of art, why was he sweeping floors instead of painting? Her grandfather probably knew all the answers to her questions, as well; unfortunately she didn't feel comfortable contacting him.

She knew her grandfather was heavily involved in the museum in Rochester, along with the New York art community as a whole. Students and collectors alike spoke his name with awe. Janessa had once felt the same admiration before she'd gone to live with him. He'd always known about her love for art and did what he could to nurture her talent from long distance.

For most of her life Janessa traveled with her parents as they worked for their magazine. Her father took photographs, and her mother wrote articles detailing wonderful sites. During that time Janessa had been homeschooled. They traveled to South Africa, Australia, the Caribbean, and Spain—finding little-known havens and bringing them to the public's attention. Sometimes they had no plumbing, fought enormous bugs, slept in crumbling buildings, and wrestled with language barriers. Other times they stayed in plush hotels, traveled on luxurious yachts in the Mediterranean, and played on secluded white sand beaches. Walter had frowned on this lifestyle, saying they were neglecting Janessa's artistic development, and he insisted she come to live with him at the age of sixteen.

Looking back, Janessa could mark this time as a critical turning point in her life. She found her grandfather difficult to get along with and impossible to please. Up until then she'd felt secure in her parents' love and the knowledge that God cared for her, but Walter was a different story. He made her feel insecure and inept. No matter what she tried she couldn't please him. She loved him and wanted to make him happy. Living in New York, she suddenly felt very alone and out of place. It was a bustling, high-paced lifestyle she'd been thrown into, and she had difficulty adapting. Trying to maintain her studies and working at her art development under her grandfather's tutelage—something she found distasteful and frustrating—brought her to the brink of a breakdown.

"But I've proven hard work can make a person successful," she reminded herself. Forcing her thoughts back to her work, Janessa dimmed the lights and flipped on the ultraviolet lamp. The ultraviolet lighting was used to pick up any inconsistencies on the canvas that weren't visible in daylight. If there were dark blotches it would indicate the painting had undergone a previous restoration. Small blue dots were dust particles. And a chartreuse haze was something she wanted to see, indicating old varnish existed on the painting and it hadn't been repaired.

Janessa looked closely at the painting. She saw no signs of

restoration, and that pleased her.

She flipped on the bright overhead lights again and snapped off the ultraviolet light. Once more her gaze wandered to all the work awaiting her attention, and it made her think of all the hard work her grandfather had demanded when she was a teen.

She had tried to satisfy him as Guy suggested, taking on anything he asked of her and silently accepting his harsh criticism. She also strove to gain Guy's admiration. Even when she couldn't detect her grandfather's approval, she had detected Guy's, and that pleased her.

Then Beth Alderman came along.

But Janessa didn't like to think of Beth, the woman who was responsible for stealing Guy's friendship and breaking his heart. Losing her one friend made Janessa question many things. By then Walter had become almost impossible to live with. He was impatient and demanding. No matter how much Janessa prayed for him, nothing changed. And this made her question whether or not she was working hard enough to get God's attention. Walter only confirmed her thoughts when he said, "God doesn't bless lazy people."

"I'm not lazy, but if I don't get my brain engaged in this project, Ted will have serious questions about my motivation," Janessa spoke into the empty room. She pressed back her glasses that tended to slip to the tip of her nose and forced herself to concentrate on Mrs. Pembroke's canvas. Seeing Guy again had her thoughts wandering in the past, but she couldn't afford to waste any more time.

On the back of the painting were stretcher bars that held the canvas taut. She quickly removed the canvas then spread the painting so it lay flat on her worktable. After pulling on gloves she grabbed a bottle of emulsion cleaner and applied a small amount with a cotton swab. The emulsion cleaner was used to remove smoke and dirt and the aged yellowed varnish that many older paintings had.

She cleaned a test spot in the corner of the canvas, expecting the painting to look lighter and more vibrant. Instead it looked cloudier.

"Strange."

She picked a second test area on the canvas, but it had the same result. It was cloudy. Then an idea struck her, something she had heard of but never seen for herself. She grabbed another bottle, this one to help remove paint. Carefully she began working away the top layer of the painting, hoping Mrs. Pembroke would forgive her as the homely yellow flowers slowly disappeared and another painting emerged.

A painting was beneath the painting!

Nothing could draw Janessa's thoughts away from her task. She worked diligently as the seconds ticked by, her fingers shaking and her breath growing shallow. The hidden painting had a dark background of a brownish black color, but in the center of the canvas was the figure of a woman with her hands crossed over her heart. As Janessa cleaned away the paint she found the woman was a young maiden, richly dressed in what looked like red brocade. The use of lighting was so exquisite that the folds of cloth looked real. The maiden's skin tone seemed to glow, and her expression could only be described as youthful and shy. Janessa had studied paintings like this one in her art history classes, and she recognized the style from the baroque period, though she'd never seen this particular piece. At first she thought it was too good to be true, but the more she worked the more she realized a treasure rested beneath her fingertips.

Below the ugly painting a masterpiece was hiding, and she

suspected it was the work of the artist Michelangelo Merisi da Caravaggio!

Janessa leaned back with a dazed expression on her face. The shrill ring of the phone on her worktable startled her. She had to force herself to answer the call.

"This is Janessa Richards," she murmured, not daring to take her gaze from the canvas in case it disappeared when she looked away.

It was Rosy. "I won't be back in today. Maybe not the rest of the week. My aunt is really sick. They just put her in the hospital, and I have to go to Syracuse. Please tell Ted for me."

"Don't worry about a thing. I'll take over your projects so he won't grumble. You'll need someone to get your mail and feed your cat. I can help if you want."

"I'm taking Fluffy with me, and my neighbor will get my mail for a few days."

"Let me help if you need anything." Once Rosy agreed, Janessa promised to pray for her aunt before ringing off.

She turned back to the masterpiece. Though her work wasn't finished and much of the old artwork still covered the canvas, it was obvious the bottom painting was exquisite. She planned to use her reference materials later to confirm her suspicions, but she was fairly certain it was created by the Italian artist, dating back to the 1500s.

And if that were the case, this little discovery would soon become public knowledge the world over. Its value was inestimable. Once the word got out, people would be clamoring to own it, legally or otherwise.

"I'm in over my head!"

Just as she was deciding whether she should contact Ted Devroe or Mrs. Pembroke first, she heard a light tap on the door. Quickly she slid a protective covering over the oil canvas.

"Yes, what is it?" she demanded nervously. When she realized how anxious she sounded she took a deep breath and forced herself to remain calm. "Did you need something?" she called and was pleased at how unaffected she sounded.

Guy stepped into the room. "I was getting ready to go home and noticed your light in here. It's well after business hours. Are you ready to quit for the evening? Maybe we could get something to eat."

Janessa darted a glance toward her worktable before turning back to Guy. "I really have a lot of work to do." More than she could handle with Rosy's projects and the new ones Ted assigned her. Even if she worked through the night rather than going home to sleep she'd still find herself behind. Unconsciously she rubbed at a tight spot in her shoulder.

Guy looked genuinely disappointed. "I thought we might be able to talk. It's been a long time since I've seen you, and you're all grown up."

Something in his tone resembled admiration, bringing a rosy glow to Janessa's cheeks. Would it hurt to meet with him? She could always come back to the museum and work a few hours more. She'd been so busy all afternoon that she hadn't even thought about food. Skipping lunch hadn't been a good idea, and the piece of toast she'd had for breakfast was a distant memory. Even though she wanted to continue working on the painting, it could wait until after a quick dinner.

As she debated how to answer Guy's offer, he moved closer to her, eyeing the covered canvas. She carefully stepped between him and the painting.

Trailing her fingers lightly over the canvas covering, she said, "Guy, do you remember how you felt when you sold your first painting and it went for more than you expected?"

He nodded, his expression curious as he watched her closely.

"This is even better. But you have to keep it confidential." Before he could ask her any questions she pulled back the covering to reveal the partially restored painting. There was still evidence of the poorly painted flowers along the edges of the canvas, but the vibrant colors of the maiden were revealed in all the rich color.

Guy stepped close and bent over the canvas. "What is this?" he asked, clearly perplexed by the dual painting.

"It's a Caravaggio! Don't you see? This painting was done over four hundred years ago, and it's assuredly priceless. A master baroque artist created this exquisite work, and I discovered it hidden under a common painting!" Realization of what she'd just said hit her, and she took a step back, suddenly feeling sick as her euphoria evaporated. Who was she to handle such a superb and inestimable piece of art? She was good at her work, but something like this should be handled by a team of professionals. What if she damaged the painting or used less preferred techniques? It would be unforgivable.

Guy seemed to sense her change in mood. "Let's forget about this for now. We should get something to eat, and you can explain exactly what we're dealing with. Then we'll come back and figure out what to do."

Janessa didn't miss his use of the word "we" and was glad he wanted to be involved, though she wasn't sure why because the painting would undoubtedly bring unwanted attention. While the museum would benefit from publicity she didn't think Guy would welcome it.

When he held out his hand, Janessa slipped her fingers between his. She knew if Rosy were there she would applaud Janessa's decision to have dinner with Guy. But she wouldn't give him the wrong impression of her. While she was a long way from outgrowing her teenage crush on him, she wouldn't ogle him as she had ten years before. This wasn't a date but a friendly gesture by a man who knew her grandfather. With a firm nod she grabbed her purse. "A slice of pizza is at the top of my list right now, and I'm buying."

Janessa's favorite pizza place was close to the museum, within walking distance, and she was glad it was a warm evening. They said little as they hurried to the restaurant, but once she was sitting in the vinyl booth she felt nervous.

Guy had followed her, carrying their separate plates of steaming pizza. He slid into the booth across from her.

"You didn't have to carry mine," Janessa offered as she reached for hers.

"I had to do something since you insisted on paying."

Janessa would have retorted that she always paid her way, but her elbow bumped her soda, sending it cascading across the table toward Guy's lap. "Oh, no! I'm so sorry! Here, let me get that!" Cola covered the table's surface and dripped steadily off the edges like a waterfall.

She'd never felt so chagrined, except when she'd tried to kiss him years earlier, but she didn't want to think of that embarrassing time—or this one. She dabbed ineffectively at the soda with her paper napkin, wishing she could rewind the moment and live it right the second time.

"Relax, Janessa." Guy grabbed her wrist, stopping her frantic swiping. A waiter approached with a big towel and soaked up the liquid.

"I'm sorry. I really feel embarrassed," she murmured, unable to look at Guy. He was probably glad to have avoided her for the past ten years.

He reached across the table and lifted her chin, forcing her to look at him. "Hey, remember when I did an interview with a society reporter for the evening news? I tripped and sprawled across the stage, and it was shown that night all across the state. That was embarrassing. Spilling a little cola between friends is nothing. Now tell me about that painting you discovered."

Janessa rewarded him with a grateful smile. "If you're sure."

"I'm sure."

It didn't take any more encouragement for her to launch into a description of her newest project. "It's a baroque period painting done by an Italian artist—probably around the year 1575. I'm going to have to double-check everything, but I'm almost a hundred percent confident it was done by Caravaggio. It matches his style perfectly."

"And no one has ever seen it? Recently, I mean? It hasn't been stolen from a museum or private collection that you know of?"

She shrugged uncertainly. "It's difficult to say. I've never heard of this piece—I've dubbed it *The Maiden*. Usually works such as his are public knowledge, unless a private collector wants to keep it a secret. I'm not certain how old the top painting was. I'm guessing about thirty years by the modern style."

"Do you think discovering it was an accident?"

Janessa blinked, surprised by his question. How could it be anything other than an accident? Mrs. Pembroke claimed it had come from the attic of her family home. But if it was only thirty years old or so, surely she would have known about it.

"Why are you asking? What do you suspect?"

Guy frowned, remaining silent for several seconds. "I'm not sure what to think except that you need to be careful. You may have discovered something that was meant to remain hidden. Or someone might have deliberately involved you in their scheme. Either way it could be dangerous."

Janessa stared wide-eyed at him. She hadn't thought about her own safety. "You don't think someone might try to steal—"

"Anything is possible. But I'm here for you, Janessa. No one will hurt you."

His statement gave her a mixed feeling of comfort and of unease. Until he said the words, she hadn't considered she might be in any danger.

೩

They returned to the museum to find Ted Devroe standing over the painting, studying the dual images. Janessa sucked in her breath ready to protest, but Guy grabbed her hand and held it firmly, stopping her from rushing forward. Why was Ted in her workroom? He didn't care about the restoration process, and he certainly didn't seek her out more than once in a single day. Even though he was the curator she felt unusually defensive when it came to *The Maiden*.

"Janessa, what is this?" Ted demanded as he frowned at Janessa's and Guy's joined hands.

Guy released her hand, but she still felt his support as she approached Ted. She remained outwardly casual though she felt tense and worried. Upon quick inspection of the painting she could see he hadn't touched it in any way except to remove the protective covering. "It's the painting Mrs. Pembroke wanted restored."

"I'm not completely ignorant, and I can see there's more to this than what you're telling me. As I recall, she brought in a painting of yellow flowers. This painting"—he motioned to the one she had discovered—"this is distinctly different. I want to know who the artist was that painted the underlying painting."

Janessa could see the dollar signs flashing in Ted's gaze and hated having to tell him the truth. While he had no interest in art, he knew a good thing when he saw one, and no doubt he would be ready to capitalize on this. She felt sorry for Mrs. Pembroke when Ted would persuade her to donate this piece to the museum. He could be very aggressive when it came to something he believed in. He would do everything in his power to turn this little gem into the moneymaker of the century.

"It's not absolute at this point, but I feel relatively confident it's a painting by Caravaggio," she answered, feeling as though he'd pulled the name from her by force.

"What period?"

"Baroque, 1575 or so."

Ted's eyes widened slightly; otherwise she saw no change in his manner. He was business as usual. "I want you to finish the restoration and forget all other projects until this one is complete. And let's keep this confidential," he added, eyeing both Janessa and particularly Guy. "We're not ready for the circus that would take place if word of this got out."

"But Mrs. Pembroke should know about—"

Ted held up his hand, giving her a dark look that silenced her. "Tell no one."

# three

Guy had to convince Janessa to allow him to stay while she worked on the painting. Getting her to agree was more difficult than he'd anticipated. She still had the gift for blushing she'd had as a teenager, but since then she'd grown more confident—and unwilling to accept anyone else's help. When he offered to straighten the room by discarding broken frames, cleaning paint splatters and filing paperwork, she refused. She said it was her job, and it wasn't fair to expect anyone else to do it for her.

Yet Guy wasn't one to sit idly by while someone else worked. Quietly, so as not to disturb her, he put the room in order without tampering or disrupting anything that looked important. Paperwork cluttered the desks. Added to that were the piles of brushes, sponges, bottles, and cloths stashed everywhere. Canvases awaiting restoration were stacked against the wall. Other paintings in varying stages of completion rested on different worktables around the room. Janessa's desk was broken and propped in place with a yardstick for its leg. He didn't know how she and Rosy accomplished anything in such a painter's nightmare.

Guy cleared the desk so he could repair the broken leg. He noticed the bottle of prescription migraine medicine and frowned. If the medication was any indication, Janessa was stressed out and working too hard. Most people would have gone home hours earlier, but Janessa worked into the night without complaint. How often did she do this? He had a feeling he wouldn't like the answer to his question.

"Guy?" Janessa had worked in silence for the last two hours. He could hear fatigue in her voice, but she didn't complain.

"Hmm?" he grunted around the two screws he held in his mouth. From his awkward position under the desk it was difficult to hold a conversation.

"Why are you here? I know you've stayed out of the art scene for the past decade. Why work at an art museum and as a janitor? You could open your own studio or teach classes—there are dozens of possibilities. I've tried to find a plausible reason. . . ." Her voice faded as she waited for him to fill in the missing answers.

Guy didn't know how to respond. Her grandfather had sworn him to secrecy, knowing she wouldn't appreciate having a watchdog hovering around her. "I've been managing a bookstore for the past few years. While I enjoy that, I also find fixing your desk a fascinating project. So I took a job here at the museum."

"Seriously, why are you staying late with me while I work tonight? I doubt you'll get overtime pay. We both know I'm not in any danger here."

Guy spat out the screws. "I'm knee-deep in old paint, and I think you have twenty-year-old paperwork on your desk marked urgent. Nothing could be more important!"

When she laughed he knew his diversionary tactic worked for now, but sometime soon all would be revealed.

He wondered if she would be laughing then.

&

Janessa wanted to keep working through the night because she was too excited about her discovery to sleep. But museum benefits couldn't be postponed because they didn't fit her schedule. If she had her way, she'd forget about the fund-raiser altogether. Dressing up and mingling with Rochester's wealthy art patrons didn't fit her idea of comfort, and she wouldn't have gone at all; but Rosy convinced her otherwise. Rosy also convinced her to buy a new dress for the event, one that was completely out of character for her.

Nothing was wrong or inappropriate with the dress, but Janessa felt as though she were wearing a costume. She felt awkward in the figure-hugging, floor-length gown made of black velvet. It accentuated her slender waist and the fairness of her skin. Thin straps with sparkling rhinestones hung from her bare shoulders. Her hair was curled and piled high on her head, she wore contacts rather than glasses, and a dusting of makeup accentuated her hazel eyes. She missed her baggy clothes and the thick glasses that made her feel safe.

She knew if Rosy had been there her friend would tell her to stop fidgeting. But Rosy hadn't been able to come to the benefit since she was with her aunt in Syracuse. It was ironic. Rosy's glamorous flamenco-style dress was hanging unused in her closet, and Janessa was sure her friend was longing to attend the benefit, while she would have given anything to be somewhere else.

She didn't like the stuffy affairs where wealthy patrons pranced around the museum and wrote out sizeable donations. She felt like an ugly duckling among so many swans. And if her grandfather was there, it would only make matters worse. She'd seen him a few times during occasions like this. Like Rosy he loved this type of event. He always made a point to talk to her though they had little to say. Janessa wanted to bridge the gap between them, but he made it clear he didn't approve of her with his harsh comments and glowering expressions. But if things became too uncomfortable she could always escape to her office. It would be a good idea anyway to check on the masterpiece.

As she watched the wealthy guests congregate to loosen their pocketbooks, Janessa wondered if her grandfather was already there amongst the crowd. Several of his paintings hung on the walls, and no doubt he would take the opportunity to bask in the spotlight for a little while. He was a major contributor to the museum, not only with his works but also with his ample pocketbook. Many times Janessa wondered if she had her job because he was such a generous contributor and on the board of directors.

"I knew you would prove me right," a deep male voice murmured close to her ear.

Janessa turned to find Ted at her elbow, dressed resplendently in a black tuxedo. While she felt awkward in her evening dress, he seemed born to wear formal attire. When he offered her a shrimp puff from the plate of a passing waiter she turned it away with a frown. Her nervous stomach revolted at the idea of food. "What have I proven?" she asked.

His dark eyes flashed with admiration as he took in her appearance. "That there really is a beautiful woman under the layers of hideous clothes you usually insist on wearing. You look incredible. Come mingle with me as I convince these fine citizens to give a million dollars to the museum. Maybe while we're mingling, you'll allow me to introduce you as my fiancée."

Janessa glanced around desperately for a means of escape. She didn't appreciate Ted's interest in her appearance or his hinting at a relationship. "Isn't there something you need me to do? I could greet people at the door or check on the refreshments. I could certainly act as a tour guide. Don't you need me to—"

Ted silenced her with a look. "Either mingle with me or

don't, but, please, Janessa, don't twitter. It ruins the glamorous look you have going."

Janessa stiffened at the rebuke. She was trying to help, not *twitter*. He usually demanded her assistance, even when she was too busy to give it. The clear lines between boss and employee seemed to cloud whenever she was around Ted. One minute he exerted his authority; the next he claimed a closer relationship with her. All the while he inserted comments into his conversation that were inappropriate for either business or a personal relationship. She didn't like his criticism.

"I'll mingle on my own, thanks. I'd hate for my unglamorous habits to annoy you," she insisted as she marched away from Ted's side. When a different waiter offered her another shrimp puff, she snatched it off the plate and popped it into her mouth.

"Janessa, wait!"

She heard Ted call after her, but she ignored him as she ducked into the crowd of people. They were more interested in socializing than studying works of art, and it was easy to lose Ted behind her.

She quickly wove through the crowd, not heeding her way as she left Ted behind her and plowed into her grandfather's side.

"Oh, sorry!"

"Janessa!" Walter's loud voice boomed out when she bumped into him. But it wasn't his hand that held her steady. She looked up to find Guy towering over her, a frown of concern puckering his brow.

"Is everything okay?" he asked softly, but she didn't have the opportunity to answer as she managed to swallow her mouthful of shrimp puff without choking on it. She'd hoped to make it through the evening without talking to Walter Richards, but now she'd have to extract herself from another uncomfortable situation.

"Hello, Grandpa—er, I mean, Walter," she stammered at his look of disapproval. He didn't like to be called anything but Walter in public.

"Still lurking in the dark, fixing other people's paintings?"

She shouldn't have hoped for him to be kind. He made her work sound so tawdry and worthless. When she didn't answer he continued, talking loudly to anyone who would listen.

"Here I stand with the two most talented young people I know, both wasting their abilities. My granddaughter sponge cleans paintings best kept in closets and attics. And Guy Langly, the once acclaimed artist I gladly took under my wing, now sweeps the floor we stand upon. Where did I go wrong?"

Some people stared; others gave an obligatory chuckle. Janessa hated being made a spectacle. Heat filled her cheeks. She still could do nothing to please him. "It was nice seeing you, Walter," she murmured, unwilling to argue as she once had. She could have told him her talent was marketable amongst thieves—would he have his granddaughter making illegal forgeries?

"Please excuse me!" She turned on her heel and hurried in the opposite direction before he could make a blustery rejoinder. By the sound of the laughter that followed her, he'd found a witty way to save the moment and reclaim everyone's adoration—except hers. It was difficult to adore a man who criticized everything and everyone.

৵

Once the laughter died down over Walter's snide comment Guy pulled his mentor aside, out of earshot of anyone who might try to listen. He was thankful Janessa hadn't heard her grandfather's remark. It had been petty and insensitive, mocking her knowledge of art. No man who loved his grandchild would speak that way. Guy had seen the hopeful expectation in Janessa's eyes as she looked up at her grandfather, but Walter had been quick to extinguish the light. Nothing had changed in the past ten years. Walter was still abrasive with his words, and Janessa was still seeking to please him. It made him angry to see how Walter ignored her need to feel secure and accepted when it was plain to him that all she wanted was her grandfather's love.

"Why did you say Janessa would be better off working with a blindfold since she has no appreciation of art? What a ridiculous thing to say, not to mention that it's untrue! Everyone heard you, and you made her look like a fool. Those comments can affect her reputation here at the museum. Don't you know how hard she works?"

Walter's shrug was indifferent. "I wasn't serious. No one thought I meant it."

Guy bristled and forced his tone to be calm even though he wanted to throttle Walter. "Listen to yourself! Whether you meant it or not, it was hurtful. You can't keep talking to her that way if you love her. She needs you to accept her, not ridicule her."

"You know nothing about it. Do everyone a favor, Guy, and stick to your job. Keep her safe."

"Keep her safe from what? Is she in danger, or are you using me to spy on her?" When Walter's face turned an alarming shade of red Guy wondered if he'd pushed too hard. "I'll keep an eye on her because she and I were always friends. I promised I would help her, and I won't go back on my word."

❧

Janessa's high heels tapped along the secluded regions of

the museum where the other partygoers hadn't wandered. She wanted to slip her feet out of the shoes and throw on a comfortable T-shirt and sweatpants. Her head throbbed, and she wished she could pull out the pins that held her hair in place. Why had she ever agreed to come? Ted didn't expect donations from her, and she hadn't helped arrange the fund-raiser. She'd thought her grandfather would be there, armed with his usual wit and sarcasm. She should have also known she would bear the brunt of his sharp words. Why did his rejection still have the power to hurt her? Unwanted tears clouded her vision, and she swiped at them in frustration.

"Lord, why can't I please him? Why can't he be proud of the work I do rather than criticizing me? I haven't seen him for so long. It should have been different!"

After walking the long corridors until she ran out of anger, Janessa found herself in a secluded alcove, lined with Renaissance art dating as far back as the year 1400. This was one of her favorite wings of the museum, and she spent her little free time here studying the beauty and idealism of a period long past. She loved the artists' use of light in their paintings as they attempted to have architectural accuracy in the background structures. In the Renaissance period they idealized the human form, making it easy to sense personality and behavior as though the artist was trying to make the painting come alive. Some of her favorites were the biblical depictions of Christ painted with Italian flair.

As she moved slowly from one familiar painting to the next the fierce ache in her head gradually subsided, and she could breathe easier. It did her no good to stay angry with her grandfather, no matter how his words hurt her. And as she stared at the old paintings of Christ—of His suffering—she began to see her situation differently. She had to forgive her grandfather once again, and forgiveness was a choice. She could never please him; yet his harsh words didn't have to affect her. Someday perhaps he would recognize her value.

She was so absorbed in the artwork that the sound of Guy's voice startled her. "Janessa, I've been searching everywhere for you. Are you all right?"

With her back to him she brushed away the last traces of tears from her cheeks before turning.

"I'm fine," she answered with a tremulous smile. "I just wanted to take a walk to clear my thoughts. Renaissance art has always been my favorite. I don't know if I ever told you."

"I remember," Guy answered softly. Rather than looking at the paintings she indicated he studied her instead. "He hasn't changed, has he? Walter says the same things now that he said ten years ago."

Janessa shrugged, turning back to the painting. "He could use a class in communicating effectively. But it doesn't matter. I rarely see him." She wondered if her words did a better job of convincing him. She'd told herself the same thing for years and still didn't believe it. Her grandfather's opinion did matter.

"He loves you," Guy insisted. "Even if he doesn't know how to show it."

Guy's comment did a strange thing to Janessa's heart. She could feel that old hope well up, but she quickly tamped it down. She wouldn't be disappointed again. What did Guy know of her grandfather's affection for her? He was just trying to make her feel better as a big brother would.

"He loves me?" Janessa gave a dry, humorless laugh. "If that's true, he has a funny way of showing it. Aside from my parents who are halfway around the world right now, Walter—as he prefers me to call him—is the only family I have, and he doesn't approve of me. I haven't set foot in his home for ten years—shortly after you disappeared. We haven't shared a single meal in as much time. Occasionally I see him, and he's always quick to remind me of what a disappointment I am to him. I thought love was supposed to be patient and kind. Love doesn't fail, does it?" She hated the tears that filled her eyes and looked away.

But Guy stepped to her side and gently turned her to face him. "Love believes all things, hopes all things, endures all things," he murmured, adding to the scripture passage she had started. He brushed away her tears. "This is God's kind of love. No matter what your grandfather does, you have to hang on to the love in your heart."

"He doesn't even like me, Guy. And I don't know why we're having this conversation. I'm not a teenager anymore, and you're not here to protect me from getting hurt."

A strange expression passed over Guy's face, and Janessa wanted to ask him about it; but a noisy group of people stepped into their secluded alcove. She stiffened when she heard Ted's voice above the others, and then a woman laughed in response to him. She knew he would be furious at finding her alone with Guy Langly after insisting she stay away from him. Though whom she spent her personal time with was her own business, she didn't want him angry with her after all the work she'd done to gain his respect. She tried to turn to see him and anyone who might be with him, but Guy blocked her view. His fingers tightened on her shoulders, and he pulled her closer to him. She found herself pressed against his chest, locked in his embrace. Before she could protest or ask him what was wrong his lips lowered over hers in a kiss.

As his lips lingered over hers Janessa forgot about Ted and the others. She no longer considered her grandfather's hurtful words. All she could think was that Guy Langly, the man she had always loved, was kissing her! She was afraid to move in case it was a leftover dream from her teenage years.

A shrill voice interrupted them, bringing Janessa back to reality with a jolt. "Guy Langly, I thought that was you!"

At the sound of the woman's voice Guy pulled back fractionally but didn't acknowledge he'd heard. Janessa peered over his shoulder to stare in horror at the small group of people watching them.

Ted glared at her, which she expected. Mrs. Pembroke stood with her fingers pressed to her lips in an effort to hide her smile. And with the group stood her grandfather, his glower matching Ted's. Janessa's heart sank as she took in his look of displeasure. Once more she'd done something to darken the Richards name in Walter's eyes. Yet when Janessa's gaze traveled to the woman who had interrupted them her eyes widened and she forgot about her grandfather.

Beth Alderman, Guy's former fiancée, stood with her hands on her hips and a pout shaping her lips as she stared at Janessa and Guy.

"Well, Guy?" Beth called out, breaking the silence that had fallen in the room.

"I'm sorry. I shouldn't have done that," Guy whispered as Janessa moved out of his embrace. He kept his arm around her waist as she took an unsteady step back.

Ted strode across the room to Janessa and took hold of her hand. "This certainly looks awkward after all I've told this group of generous benefactors." He laughed, turning back to the group. Janessa had no choice but to follow since he had a viselike grip on her hand. "Everyone, this is Janessa Richards, my special girl. She's personally responsible for making many of the fine oil paintings shine with new life. She takes something old and unattractive and turns it into a piece worthy of our enjoyment."

Janessa tried to tug her hand free, but Ted wouldn't release her. Instead he pulled her forward so her shoulder bumped his. He placed a steadying arm around her waist. She wished it were Guy who still held her.

"I've been telling everyone, *darling*, that you and I have a special arrangement. Even though we work at the museum together we have a much closer relationship."

He appeared at ease, but Janessa sensed Ted's anger and discomfort. She had no idea why he'd said such things to these people or what benefit there would be to him. Why would he tell her grandfather he had a relationship with her unless he hoped it might help his career?

"Ted, I don't think—"

"Darling, Mrs. Pembroke here is asking about her painting. I told her we are working to ensure she'll be very pleased." At the mention of the painting Janessa stiffened. Mrs. Pembroke's dull painting was actually a masterpiece, and the woman knew nothing of the treasure she owned.

As Mrs. Pembroke moved closer, Janessa noticed that Beth detached herself from the group to join Guy. She reminded Janessa of a panther stalking its prey.

"How pretty you look!" Mrs. Pembroke exclaimed, bringing Janessa's attention back with a jerk. "I've been wondering how my painting is coming along. Have you had a chance to take a peek yet?"

Ted hugged Janessa to his side and gave her shoulder a warning squeeze. "She's been so busy, Mrs. Pembroke. I'm sure you know these things take time."

Janessa wanted to tell Mrs. Pembroke of her amazing discovery, but then she remembered what such an announcement would cause. Most of the people at the fund-raiser would recognize the name of Caravaggio, and it would create a sensation if they knew one of his paintings had been hidden in Mrs. Pembroke's attic. Not only would it bring attention to the museum, but Mrs. Pembroke would also receive unwanted interest.

"Oh, yes, yes, my dear!" Mrs. Pembroke nodded as she patted Janessa's arm with affection. "You take your time. And just between you and me I hope you can do a miracle. Those flowers are awful!"

Janessa thought of the canvas and how the flowers were nearly removed from the surface. "I'm sure you'll be surprised," she responded.

"Enough of this talk, ladies! Let's finish our tour. Janessa, darling, stay with me. I'm sure your grandfather would love to hear your impressions on some of our newer acquisitions. I've told him how close you and I have become, and I-was surprised you hadn't told him yourself. I assured him I never let you out of my sight," Ted added with an edge to his words. Janessa glanced over her shoulder and knew her grandfather had heard every word as Ted intended. What she didn't understand was why Ted was putting on this display. He snaked his arm around Janessa's waist and pulled her toward the corridor.

She knew without looking that Guy and Beth wouldn't be joining the group.

≈

"What are you doing here?" Guy glowered at Beth as the others moved away from the alcove. He knew his actions would speak volumes to Janessa and she'd jump to all the wrong conclusions. Unfortunately he couldn't go after her since Beth had effectively cornered him.

"Don't look so stern, Guy. You know I don't like it when

you're upset with me," she answered as she draped her arm around his neck.

Guy jerked away from her and put as much distance between them as possible, but she quickly closed the space between them.

"I don't know you anymore, Beth! We haven't seen each other for ten years so you can't expect me to be taken in so easily. Last I heard you were going to marry a plastic surgeon who could make all your dreams come true."

"Well, that didn't work out," she snapped, letting her hands rest at her hips.

As the room seemed to grow stuffier, Guy knew it was time to retreat. Within five minutes Beth was able to revive all the anger and frustration he'd worked for years to deal with. He wouldn't let her step in and try to ruin his life again. "It was nice seeing you, Beth. I wish you well."

"Not so fast!" As he tried to walk away Beth snagged his arm. "I'm here for a reason. You and I were good together, and when we broke up both of our careers ended. Let's help each other. I want to start modeling again. I'm sure you need some inspiration to begin painting. We could be a team once more." She batted her eyelashes at him, and Guy knew she was after more than a business relationship.

"Not a chance," he answered grimly. Though Beth was as beautiful now as she had been ten years ago he knew she was dangerous—pretending to be soft and gentle while hiding her vicious claws. She'd already broken his heart; he wouldn't let her get close enough to go a second round.

Beth laughed, a low sultry sound that made every muscle in his neck tense. "I'm not a patient woman, and I know what I want. I'm sure you remember how I always get my way. This isn't over—not by a long shot."

Guy watched her swagger out of the room, letting her get the last word. It was true she usually got what she wanted and discarded those she was finished with. At one time he believed she was a good Christian girl and that he wanted to spend the rest of his life with her. Then he learned how shallow her faith ran.

She fooled him once, but she wouldn't do it again.

# four

Janessa had to jog to keep up as Ted led her down the darkened hallway of the administration portion of the museum. After making polite excuses to his guests he'd taken hold of Janessa and quickly ushered her away from the party. She stumbled in her high heels, but Ted was in no mood for chivalry. Janessa could only pray he wasn't so angry she would lose her job.

She didn't need a lecture from him about the propriety of kissing someone where she worked. She knew better, and until Guy reappeared in her life she'd never been tempted. Though the kiss had been everything she ever dreamed of, she was already regretting it. Guy had apologized. After she allowed her love to pour into that kiss he'd trammeled her hopes with a few simple words, and she felt like a fool. Had she disappointed him? Was that why he regretted kissing her?

Wordlessly Ted opened his office and flipped on the lights inside. He stepped aside to let her enter then shoved the door closed behind them. Janessa felt like a tardy schoolgirl visiting the principal's office.

"Why did you kiss Langly after I asked you to stay away from him?" Ted circled his desk and sat in the plush leather seat. He indicated the chair across from him, but she chose to stand, bristling with indignation.

He didn't care that she was kissing someone in the dark corners of the museum. He was mad because Guy was the recipient of those kisses! She wanted to argue that it was none of his business, but Ted's temper was a tricky matter. If she incited his anger he might fire her.

Janessa took a deep breath. "Tell me instead why you told everyone we have a relationship. You indicated it's much closer than a working relationship," she demanded softly once her temper was reined in. "It's not the truth."

"I thought you could use a little encouragement in that area. You know I've been interested in you—"

"You've been interested in changing me. Never has a boss nitpicked about my clothes, my hairstyle, even my posture! You approve of my work, but you're not interested in me, Ted, not romantically."

Ted looked startled. "That's not true! I've thought long and hard about this, and I can't find anyone who would make a better wife for me. You're a faithful churchgoer, and aside from that little display this evening your behavior is beyond reproach. You do everything I ask of you. You go out of your way to help others. I've watched you closely, and I know what I'm talking about. You're a hard worker and a generous, godly woman. I only want to help you look better, like now, Janessa." He motioned to her slim black dress. "Tonight I couldn't find anything wrong with your appearance even if I tried. You look ravishing."

His intense approval brought a blush to Janessa's cheeks along with uneasiness in her heart. She had no idea Ted felt so strongly—enough to consider her a potential wife.

"I should fire Langly. I don't like him or the effect he has on you."

"What effect? He's not interested in me—just as you aren't either." When Ted tried to protest, Janessa held up her hand to silence him. "I hate to disappoint you, Ted, but tomorrow I'm going back to the brown skirts and baggy sweaters. And if you really like me as you say, this news shouldn't upset you—as it obviously does," she stated dryly when he curled his lip in distaste. "And next time please don't imply there's a cozy relationship between us when there's not. You're the curator. I restore paintings. We have nothing more than a good working relationship, and your insinuations could make things difficult for me. It wasn't honest."

Ted sat back in his chair, saying nothing, his arms folded over his chest. Janessa was again struck by how different they were. How could he consider asking her to be his wife? She knew he approved of her talent for restoring paintings. Did his interest have something to do with her work?

She wasn't sure where her thoughts were leading, but she suddenly felt suspicious. "You don't really want me for your wife, but you want my grandfather to think otherwise. Why? Is it because of my work for the museum or because he's on the museum's board?" She paused, studying his grim expression. "What's going on? Why are you acting so strange? The only thing that has changed is my discovery of the painting." She paused and studied his closed expression. "This couldn't have anything to do with Mrs. Pembroke's painting, could it?"

Ted laughed, but it was a dry, humorless sound. "You mean the Caravaggio? I made a few discreet phone calls, and it's probably a forgery. The painting underneath is no more valuable than the cheap flowers painted on top. At least you didn't say anything to Mrs. Pembroke—and make sure you don't talk to her about this! She doesn't need to know anything. But now we have to figure out what to do about her missing yellow flowers that were scraped from the canvas. Two worthless paintings—what a waste."

Janessa studied Ted's impassive expression and began to feel uneasy. Something about his words didn't ring true. Why would anyone paint such a masterful forgery and then cover it with an amateur's hideous artwork? Why did it seem he was evading her questions? Was something going on with the painting that both Ted and her grandfather knew about?

"Stop asking questions and drawing conclusions to something you know nothing about, Janessa. I don't like being such a dictator, but you have to listen to me. Stick to what you're good at—restoring paintings. And stay away from Langly."

&

Guy had searched for Janessa at the benefit, but she seemed to have disappeared as Beth did once she was finished with him. Guy wanted to explain to Janessa what the kiss had been all about; but she was nowhere to be found, and he suspected she was upset. Once he realized Ted was gone, as well, it didn't take a genius to know Janessa was with the curator. He could only hope she would be careful. Guy felt uneasy knowing she was alone with Ted Devroe and he could do nothing about it. When an hour passed and Ted had returned to the benefit, but Janessa was still absent, Guy assumed it was safe to go home. She had probably ducked out a back door in hopes of avoiding him.

Now he stared at the blank canvas propped on the easel before him and muttered under his breath. He hadn't picked up a paintbrush in ten years, not since Beth had taught him the cruel lesson about love. He hadn't been drawn to the passion that once consumed his days and even wondered if he would ever paint again. Now he knew with a certainty he would paint again just as he knew God would heal the hurts he'd suffered.

The white canvas drew him as it had so long ago, begging him to bring life to the image born in his mind. Fighting the gift God had given him was like fighting the desire to breathe. He had to do it. With only a minimal amount of hesitation he picked up a brush and began shaping the image of the person who was often in his mind lately.

Just as he started to lose himself in his work he heard a firm tap on his apartment door. Guy was tempted to ignore it, but the sharp sound had already broken his concentration. With a sigh he put down his brush and hurried toward the door.

Walter Richards, with his customary scowl, stood in the doorway. "Can you see now why she needs protection?" Still dressed in formal attire, he brushed past Guy into the apartment. He gave the cramped surroundings a cursory inspection before turning back to Guy. "You have to do something. She can't marry that buffoon."

"I didn't hear anyone mention marriage," Guy answered. He wasn't surprised to see Walter. They'd both heard Ted Devroe's announcement that he had a close relationship with Janessa. He could understand Walter's concern after having met Ted. He was a controlling perfectionist who thought he could make unreasonable demands of Janessa. What Walter didn't know was that she couldn't be in love with Ted—not after the way she'd returned Guy's kiss.

"You never know what might occur if we're not careful. He's smooth—too smooth for my liking. He may not have mentioned marriage, but I know he wants her for his bride."

Guy went into the open kitchen and poured two glasses of purified water. "When I agreed to your plan, Walter, I agreed to protect her from physical harm because you were under the impression she was in danger. I'm her friend, and I care about her a great deal. But I won't manipulate her personal life."

"And yet I caught you kissing her. That looked personal to me!" Walter slammed his fist down on the counter, rattling the glasses. "No! I won't have it! I've worked with Ted Devroe long enough to know what manner of man he is. He'll ruin her."

"Do you really suspect she may be in danger, or are you just using me to spy on her?" Guy asked again calmly. Aside from finding the priceless painting, he saw no reason why Janessa was in harm's way. If word got out about the painting, that might be a different story. Many people would be after such an exquisite piece, and he'd hate to see her caught in the middle. For once he agreed with Ted Devroe about keeping it quiet. "In all fairness to Janessa, I doubt she'd consider a marriage offer from him. She's not blind to his ways."

"But what if he forces her? You heard his threats—and I took them as threats. He wanted to make sure I know he's after my granddaughter."

Walter strode into the living room where Guy had his easel propped near the large picture window. Guy held his breath, hoping Walter wouldn't take notice of the new painting taking shape. He wasn't interested in being critiqued after so many years away from his craft. But Walter didn't seem to notice the painting as he stood looking down at the city lights. Guy had the chance to study his mentor while he waited for him to respond. The years hadn't been kind to him, and he looked more haggard and even sadder than Guy remembered. Most people wouldn't understand what could make him sad. He was a successful artist, wealthy and highly respected in his field. Prints of his paintings hung in homes all over the world. Yet he had no relationship with his son and daughter-in-law who traveled together for their work. If Guy remembered correctly, Walter had severed the relationship when they refused to do his bidding. And now his only granddaughter didn't want to be near him. He'd seen the hurt on her face when Walter criticized her at the museum's benefit.

"I just want you to help me, Guy. Call it spying if you want. I don't want to see her make the same mistakes I've made in my life, and I don't want her to marry the wrong person."

"And how do we ever know who is right and who is wrong?" Guy asked, thinking of Beth. She'd seemed right for him in every way until he realized it had been a facade. Even at the benefit that evening, after ten years of separation, he still found her beautiful. She'd clung to him, whispering persuasively in hopes of reconciliation. He was thankful he hadn't lost his senses and agreed to what she wanted. No way could he go back to the pain he had worked through.

"I know Ted Devroe is trouble, and I don't want Janessa to have anything to do with him. You said you'd help me, and I want you to keep them apart. Whatever it takes." Walter's gaze challenged him to back away from the task. Yet he had to know Guy wouldn't quit on this. He may have quit everything else, but he would see this through.

Walter gave him a nod of approval, evidently sensing Guy's unspoken commitment.

"I saw Beth Alderman at the benefit tonight." He paused, eyeing him speculatively. "She won't interfere in your job, will she?"

"No, sir," Guy answered firmly. Seeing Beth again had been difficult, and he admitted he'd taken advantage of Janessa to protect himself. When he heard Beth's familiar laugh it had been like a jab to his abdomen. He hadn't wanted to face her, and Janessa had been there, only a breath away. So he kissed her, to prove to Beth that he was no longer brooding over a relationship long expired.

He'd expected Janessa to be surprised, even offended by the kiss, but he hadn't anticipated the flood of emotion he experienced. It was like a jolt of electricity running through his veins, and if he closed his eyes and thought about it he could probably feel it all again. But he wasn't ready to analyze those emotions, and he certainly wasn't going to divulge any of his thoughts to Walter. He needed time to think about it and pray, asking God what it all meant.

Walter turned away from Guy to stare down at the canvas that was no longer blank but had a long way to go before it was finished. He studied the form and the careful brush strokes for long moments, taking in every detail and no doubt forming a lengthy criticism. Guy braced himself for the harsh comment he knew was coming, but Walter surprised him.

"It's good to have you back, Guy."

# five

"Where's the painting? Where's the painting!"

Janessa stepped into her workroom early the next morning, even though it was Saturday. She'd spent a restless night and decided the best thing to take her mind off all her troubling thoughts was work—except her work had vanished.

The door to the room was locked as usual when she arrived, and very few people had a key. After a quick perusal she could confidently say nothing else was out of place. Whoever entered the room had known about the painting. And that meant one of three people had been there—her, Ted, or Guy. Rosy had already left for Syracuse before Janessa had discovered the Caravaggio.

*The Maiden*, Janessa's name for it, was missing. If it truly was worthless as Ted claimed, why would anyone steal it?

"I need to calm down. Perhaps Mrs. Pembroke came for her painting, and Ted had to give her the Caravaggio." Or what she *thought* was a Caravaggio. Despite his claims it was a forgery, Janessa wasn't convinced.

She hurried from the room, careful to lock it behind her, and went to Ted's office. It was early, but there was every possibility he was there. He often started his day well before the museum opened, and after the benefit last night he probably wanted a little more time to get everything in order for the day.

Janessa's steps slowed as she tried to figure out who would steal the painting. Over a hundred people wandered through the museum during the benefit. Any one of them could have broken into her workroom and stolen the masterpiece.

Yet none of them knew it was there, except perhaps her grandfather.

As she approached Ted's office she could hear his muffled voice, and he sounded angry. She moved closer, wondering whom he was talking with. Pausing just outside the door, she tried to decide if she should knock or wait until he was off the phone. He already sounded agitated; her arrival would make matters worse.

She glanced down at her gray slacks and cream-colored blouse. At least he couldn't criticize her wardrobe selection—nothing baggy or unsightly. She was dressed conservatively, *like a deacon's wife*, she thought with a grimace.

"I don't care what you think! Just find someone! I need someone over here now to take it," Ted growled.

Janessa nudged the door open a little farther with her toe as she held her breath. Her mother taught her that listening at doors only brought more trouble, but she chose to ignore that lesson now. Instinctively she knew this had something to do with the painting.

"It's hot, and it needs to go. No! I need you to deal with it and quickly. Something like this doesn't show up every day, and I'm a nervous wreck because of it!" He slammed down the phone.

Janessa sagged against the wall, wondering what she should do—confront Ted? Should she call the authorities or forget she overheard the conversation? She had no proof Ted planned to sell the Caravaggio. His conversation made her suspicious, but what if he was talking about selling his house? Or a car? How did she know he wanted to sell the painting?

Before she could move or announce her arrival Ted's door swung open.

"Janessa!" His gaze narrowed on her flushed face, and she knew she was in trouble. "How long have you been listening at my door?"

"Where's the Caravaggio? I came in early this morning, and it's gone!"

A tight smile crept over Ted's lips, but the humor never reached his dark eyes as he stared down at her. "Don't worry, Janessa. I brought the painting into my office because I expect Mrs. Pembroke to stop over. I figured it would be easier to explain the situation in the privacy of this room where she can see the canvas for herself."

"When she arrives I'd like to talk to her, as well. She should understand the steps I went through to discover the painting underneath. I'm sure it will be quite a shock to know her original painting is gone."

Ted shook his head firmly. "It won't be necessary for you to talk to her. As you know, her painting is not entirely gone." At Janessa's puzzled look he opened a file that sat on his desk and picked up a snapshot of the yellow-flowered painting. She always took "before" photos of a canvas when she started the restoration process.

"I want you to recreate the original painting from the photograph."

"I couldn't!" Janessa knew she could recreate it precisely so even the artist would question whether he had painted it himself, but she wasn't about to tell Ted that.

He gave her a placating smile. "Don't misunderstand me. I don't want you to deceive the woman. It's merely a gift. Of course we'll tell her it isn't the original. She said herself the painting wasn't very desirable to begin with. This way she'll walk away with two paintings. And if the Caravaggio turns out to be an original, which I still doubt, she'll be even better off."

His explanation sounded plausible. He wanted to maintain good relations with one of the museum's most generous benefactors. Yet she couldn't help being suspicious after overhearing his telephone conversation. Was he planning to sell the painting and pass off a forgery to Mrs. Pembroke? Janessa couldn't imagine a more gentle or kind person than the little lady. Mrs. Pembroke baked cookies for her neighbors and helped at the local animal shelter. Not only was she a long-time supporter of the museum, Janessa had worked with her on numerous occasions. Many of the paintings in her home had been restored, and some were quite valuable. Yet none was anything like the masterpiece Janessa discovered beneath the painting of yellow flowers.

"You're going to sell the Caravaggio, aren't you? You're trying to convince me it's a fake when I'm almost a hundred percent sure it's authentic. Then you're going to pass off a freshly painted forgery to a sweet little lady. How can you do this, Ted? You're supposed to be a man of God. How can you do this?"

"Mrs. Pembroke isn't as sweet as you think, Janessa. What do you really know about her? Not much, right? Do you realize you might be accusing the wrong person? Do you understand what you're accusing me of?" His lips pressed into a thin line, and his eyes narrowed dangerously.

Janessa swallowed, finding it hard to breathe around the sudden tightness in her throat. Was she encouraging him to fire her? If she continued with the accusations she'd probably find herself unemployed. "I–I'm accusing you of selling a painting."

"You're accusing the curator of Rochester's Museum of Fine Art of stealing—not just selling—another person's painting. You have only theories and no proof."

Janessa stared at him as silence stretched between them. Here it was. She was about to lose the most important thing in her life next to her faith. "Are you going to fire me?"

Ted's frown melted into a smile as he crossed the room. Janessa stiffened when he gently clasped her shoulders and gave her a playful squeeze. "You've been watching too many spy thrillers on television. I'm not the bad guy here, Janessa. I'm just a museum curator trying to figure out the best thing to do in a sticky situation. Mrs. Pembroke entrusted us with a painting of yellow flowers, and you destroyed that painting." When she tried to protest he pressed his finger to her lips. "It doesn't matter that another painting was hidden beneath it. What matters is that Mrs. Pembroke is coming to get her painting, and I have to explain everything to her. So I'm asking you—pleading with you—to cooperate. I need you to paint a copy of Mrs. Pembroke's flowers. Put your name on it so there's no question that it's not the original. Then trust me to handle this in the most straightforward way the circumstances will allow. Do it my way, and no one will get hurt. I promise."

"Hurt?"

Ted shrugged and released her shoulders. With a placating smile he strode to his desk and picked up a paper, indicating their meeting was coming to a close. "I used the wrong word. No one will be *upset*. Okay, Janessa? Work with me? You need this job, and I need your expertise." He glanced up and met her gaze briefly. When she didn't immediately answer he raised his brow in a gesture of impatience. "Well?"

"You'll tell Mrs. Pembroke the truth?"

"Allow me to handle this, Janessa. Everything will come to light when the time is right."

❧

Janessa painted the forgery of Mrs. Pembroke's yellow flowers according to Ted's instruction. The work went quickly as she copied the photo onto canvas. The design was simple and required very little time or effort. She longed to make the vase a smoother shape and add touches that would improve the image, but she refrained and kept the copy exactly like the original. Once she finished the painting, there was no way to tell the original from the forgery except for the small *J* she painted in the lower right corner. The colors leaped freshly from the canvas as though it had just been restored.

As she was putting her supplies away she heard a light tap on her workroom door, and Guy slipped into the room. Janessa caught her breath, not expecting to see him. After their kiss and his quick dismissal she wasn't prepared to face him. She had spent the last hours thinking of the Caravaggio and the new painting she'd made for Mrs. Pembroke. She hadn't thought about what she should say or how she might act around Guy when she faced him again, and now that he stood before her she was uncomfortable.

"I'm surprised to see you here on a Saturday. I thought Joe worked the weekends," she said evenly as she cleaned her paintbrushes. Joe was the "retired" custodian who had come in every weekend Janessa had worked for the museum and longer. He was a quiet man who kept to himself, but he always had a kind word for her. She would have found Joe much easier to face than Guy. She kept her gaze on her work and was glad when neither her voice nor her hands shook.

"I just wanted to make sure you're okay. When I went by your apartment—"

She looked up at him in surprise. "You went to my home? But why?" If he wanted to apologize again for kissing her, she didn't want to hear it.

"To make sure you're safe," he said simply, not taking his

gaze from her face. "And because I wanted to see you."

Janessa frowned, expecting him to say something about the kiss or the way he'd abandoned her last evening to be with Beth. She felt let down that he wasn't interested in discussing those things, even though she wasn't ready herself.

"You think I might be at risk because of the Caravaggio?"

Guy moved his shoulders in a slight shrug, but it was answer enough for Janessa. "Well, I think it's ridiculous. Ted thinks the painting is worthless, and he's giving it back to Mrs. Pembroke along with this copy of her original painting." She motioned to the canvas of the garish yellow flowers she'd just finished. Once it dried she would frame it with a nice oak border, and Mrs. Pembroke would be thrilled, if not a little perplexed, by the second painting.

"That's a forgery?" Guy asked, incredulous.

"I prefer to call it a replacement painting. Ted could hardly give her the original."

"And what about the Caravaggio? Has Ted asked you to paint a replacement of that one, as well?"

"No, he hasn't. I don't know why you're being so suspicious, Guy. Ted has no alternative but to give Mrs. Pembroke her painting, and he thought it would be a nice gesture for her to receive this one. She'll know it's a copy. He assured me."

Guy didn't look convinced.

"I asked him what he plans to do with the painting, and he promised to give it back to Mrs. Pembroke. He's the curator, after all."

"And you believe him?"

Did she? Janessa had to admit she'd been suspicious, and it was easy to believe the worst of Ted when he'd taken the painting to his office. His phone conversation did nothing to bolster her trust, but his explanation seemed sound.

As far as motives went, she should be questioning Guy about his. He wasn't interested in the Caravaggio, of course, but why had he kissed her then spent the evening with Beth?

"You shouldn't even be in here, Guy. Ted warned me to stay away from you after our—" She faltered, unable to mention their interrupted kiss. Was he seeing his old flame again that night? It didn't matter, she tried to convince herself. Guy could see whomever he wanted, and she had no say. That fact shouldn't have bothered her as much as it did—almost as much as it hurt when she watched Guy fall in love with Beth the first time ten years earlier. "I have so much work to do. If you came in today just to check on me, you don't need to worry. I'm okay." Her voice was firm, allowing no argument.

"I'm not just checking on you. I was wondering if you might have dinner with me sometime. We could go someplace quiet to talk."

Was he asking her on a date? Her heart pounded at the thought of it, but she pressed it aside. "That might be nice. Sometime."

Guy looked as if he wanted to say something more, but he didn't. "All right, I'll go. But if you need anything, I plan to stay in the building," he assured her as he backed through the doorway.

Janessa returned to the stack of canvases piled against the wall. She forced her thoughts on her work to keep her mind from picturing his blond good looks, his twinkling blue eyes, the gentle way he had kissed her and how his gaze seemed to caress her. No matter how much work she had, she had a feeling it would be impossible for her to think of anything but Guy.

"Janessa?"

She glanced up, startled by his voice. She thought he'd

already left and hoped he couldn't somehow know what she'd been thinking. "Yes?"

"Don't work too hard. It's not what you do, but who you are that makes people like you."

"Maybe in your world, Guy, but not in mine," she replied softly.

Guy's words hung in her thoughts as she worked through the afternoon and into the evening. As fingers of pain gripped her spine from too many hours bent over her worktable, she wished she could believe what he said. Her parents had taught her that love was unconditional, and she'd always felt secure with them. But her grandfather had given her a real world lesson. He showed her that respect had to be earned and the only way to get people to care was to work, work, work! And sometimes hard work wasn't enough to ensure lasting respect. One false move—like choosing to go to the university instead of becoming an artist—and the respect vanished.

The shrill cry of the telephone broke into Janessa's thoughts, and she snatched up the receiver, thankful for the interruption.

"Janessa! I knew you'd be at work. I didn't even try to call you at home," Rosy said.

"Rosy! How is your aunt? Is everything okay?"

"She's better and out of the hospital, but I'm going to stay with her for a few days. You don't mind working alone?"

"I miss your constant chatter, for sure." Rosy's answering laugh made her grin.

"How was the benefit last night? Did you wear the dress?"

Janessa didn't want to answer any questions about the benefit since it seemed like such a dismal failure as far as she was concerned. She probably would have been better off wearing her paint smock and avoiding Guy's heart-stopping kiss. "It was a successful evening for the museum, I'm sure."

"Hmm, a cryptic answer. You know I won't be satisfied with that. If I had more time I'd ask you a million questions, but I have to go. Take care of yourself, Janessa."

"You, too, Rosy."

Out of habit Janessa punched one of the line buttons on her phone to make sure the call was disconnected. The museum's telephone system needed updating, and her phone wasn't always reliable. As she pressed the button she accidentally picked up a conversation on another line. Before she could discreetly hang up a few words caught her attention.

"You're certain it's a Caravaggio? If it's authentic, then we'd better move quickly."

Janessa sucked in her breath. It sounded like her grandfather, and he was talking about *The Maiden*!

"I agree, and I thought you'd have come for it by now," Ted responded. "The longer it sits in my office, the more risks I take."

Janessa's heart sank with Ted's words. He did plan to sell it after he promised her he wouldn't. Even worse, her grandfather was involved. The thought made her sick. It seemed impossible. He was harsh and critical, but he wasn't an art thief! And how could Ted, a man professing to be a Christian, be lured away? She knew the "enemy of men" was just waiting to trap anyone he could catch, and both Ted and Walter had fallen into the snare. Should she go to the police? She had no evidence to prove her own grandfather and the museum's curator were guilty of a future theft. Would the authorities laugh at her in disbelief? What if she was wrong—would she harm Ted's career? Would she push her grandfather away forever?

She pressed the button to disconnect the line on her phone carefully, so they wouldn't know she'd overheard the call, then set the receiver back in its cradle. There would probably be an audible click on the line, but she prayed Ted would blame it on the dated system.

After hearing Ted discussing the painting, Janessa no longer wanted to be in the museum. She needed time alone so she could pray for direction. If only her parents were around to advise her! It would cost too much to explain everything through a long distance call. And if either of her parents were distracted by their project details, she'd never get a helpful answer anyway.

Tossing aside her smock, she grabbed her purse. The wall clock caught her attention, and she stared at it in disbelief. It was already ten o'clock in the evening!

With her thoughts on Ted's phone conversation, Janessa hurried out the door. She didn't think to say good-bye to Guy until the door closed behind her. Most likely he'd gone home hours earlier. *To be with Beth*, a hurtful little voice whispered in her ear. Janessa pushed the thought away. She didn't blame him for not saying good-bye to her either, after the way she'd brushed him off. He was her friend, and she'd treated him shabbily when she should have confronted him about the kiss and the confusion she felt because of it.

She hurried across the parking lot, anxious to get home. It wasn't far to her apartment, but she didn't like to walk alone so late at night. She quickened her pace, darting through the maze of parked cars. Behind her she heard the sound of footsteps echoing on the pavement. Her heart thumped louder.

She willed herself to move swiftly and calmly, hoping the other person was searching for his car. A number of cars were still in the lot.

"God, protect me," she whispered, wishing she didn't feel so nervous. She'd never been scared to be alone before she had found the Caravaggio. Now the shadows seemed to jump out at her.

The footsteps were behind her, closing fast. Janessa didn't dare turn around. She quickened her steps to a trot just as someone's gloved hand reached out and grabbed her arm, jerking her to a stop.

Janessa would have screamed, but the stranger's other hand closed over her mouth. He jerked her backward until she fell against him.

"Give me the painting," the man hissed into her ear.

"What painting? I don't know what you're talking about!" Janessa stammered against his hand.

"I think you do!" he growled in response.

Janessa twisted in his hold, trying to get a good look at her attacker. She expected to see Ted, but she didn't recognize this man. His face was shadowy in the darkness, but instinctively she knew she'd never seen him before. How did this stranger know about the masterpiece, if that was the painting he wanted?

"Do you understand?" the man ground out as his fingers bit into her cheeks. "Give me the painting, or you'll be sorry!"

Janessa nodded faintly. Her heart pounded in her chest, and her lungs felt as if they might burst. On an impulse she stomped as hard as she could on his foot. When he loosened his grasp with a grunt she jabbed her elbow into his stomach. He jerked his hand from her mouth, and she screamed as she struggled to run away from him.

"Help! Help me, someone!" Her sleeve tore in the stranger's grasp as she fought herself loose.

"Janessa!"

It was Guy! She ran toward the sound of his voice. "Guy,

help me!" The words caught on a sob in her throat. She gasped for breath and willed her feet to move faster. She could hear the stranger darting between the cars, but she couldn't tell if he was chasing after her or running in the opposite direction. When she turned to see for sure, she lost her balance and slammed against a parked car, striking her forehead against it.

Strong arms closed around her, and she fought instinctively to be free. "Let me go!"

"Janessa, stop! It's me, Guy. You're safe now."

The sound of his voice made the fear and tension flow out of Janessa, and she sagged against his chest. "It was awful. He came out of nowhere." She couldn't stop the sobs that tried to choke her.

"A mugger?"

She shook her head. "No. He wanted me to give him the painting. I know he wants the Caravaggio. Guy, what do you think this is about? How could he know?"

His arms tightened around her. "I don't know, but I think it's time to call the police."

ॐ

After an hour of thorough questioning by the police, Janessa was ready to go home. The police offered to send an extra patrol through the neighborhood, but when Guy asked for even more protection, they said it wasn't possible to provide the security he wanted.

Janessa's forehead felt bruised from colliding with the parked car, and a full-blown migraine had taken root. The icepack provided by a kind officer helped, but she knew she'd have a souvenir in the form of a purple goose egg when she awoke in the morning. That is, if she could sleep. It seemed a percussion ensemble had taken residence in her head, and every muscle in her body ached.

She was thankful Guy sat beside her and held her hand the entire time while she explained to the officer about the hidden painting and the ensuing events that led up to the stranger's warning in the parking lot. The officer wrote down the information and to Janessa's surprise didn't balk at her suspicions. She hated mentioning her grandfather's name, but she had doubts about him after hearing his conversation with Ted.

Once the questioning was over and a report was filed Guy walked her outside. The air was cold for late April, and she couldn't help shivering. Her sleeve was torn, and she didn't have a jacket.

When he slipped his arm around her shoulders for warmth she leaned into his side. She didn't think about her confusion or vulnerability where he was concerned. She wanted to be close to him and draw on the comfort he offered. Without Guy, the stranger may have hurt her.

"You're never alone, Janessa," he murmured.

"Yes, I'm glad you were there when I needed you."

Guy shook his head. "I'm not talking about me. I meant God. He's always there for you, watching over you."

"Do you really feel that way? I believe in God, but so often I don't feel worthy of His love or His favor. There're so many people and problems in this world—why would He take time with me?" She thought of her grandfather's words from long ago that always hung at the back of her thoughts. *Not even God gives favors, Janessa. You have to work hard if you want anything.*

"I have to believe it, or else I wouldn't have a reason to live. God is more than a taskmaster or ruling judge sitting on a heavenly throne. How could He pick favorites by caring for one person while ignoring another? He doesn't do that. He's a loving parent who wants a part in our lives."

Janessa sighed, trying to take in all he said though her head pounded furiously. "I want to believe you, but for some reason God seems more like my grandfather than a loving father. Doesn't He want us to live without sin and do good works? I can't please Walter. How could I ever please God?"

Guy turned her toward him, cupping her cheek gently with his hand. She stared up at him, thankful for his strength and his willingness to help her—even if his heart probably still belonged to Beth. For the moment she could imagine they were the only ones in the world—with no strangers in the parking lot, disapproving grandfathers, or mystery paintings. Janessa closed her eyes, savoring the touch of his warm fingers against her cool cheek. She wished he would kiss her again. Having him close was worth the confusion she'd deal with later.

"No matter what you do or how you think, God loves you. You don't have to worry about pleasing Him because He's already pleased with you."

Janessa longed to believe him, and yet something held her back. She'd always believed God was sitting on His throne, waiting for her to make a mistake so He could teach her a lesson. Everything Guy said went against the old Sunday school lessons she'd learned. Hadn't God destroyed Sodom and Gomorrah? Flooded the earth? Punished the Israelites? Janessa didn't want him to be angry with her, as well.

"Please, Guy, just take me home," she said wearily, not wanting to think about it any longer.

Guy's arm tightened around her shoulders. "I can't do that."

She looked at him curiously with a frown puckering her brow. "You can't?"

"No. I don't want you staying alone, and it wouldn't be right for you to stay at my place. Do you have anywhere else you can go?"

Rosy was away, and no one else would want to find her on the doorstep so late. "There's nowhere."

"Let me take you to your grandfather's."

Janessa stiffened and pulled away. "No, thanks! It would be better for me to bed down at the bus station than sleep on his sofa. I'll be fine on my own. It was just a warning." Her words were brave, but the memory of the stranger's attack played through her mind. What if he appeared at her apartment with another warning?

"Then I have only one alternative, Janessa. I'm taking you to my sister's."

# six

Janessa tried to protest, but Guy would hear none of it. She didn't want to inconvenience his sister by appearing at her house so late. Yet Guy said Sara was like her in that she wanted to help others no matter what the inconvenience was to her. The compliment made her feel good, but she still wasn't convinced his sister would agree.

Sara greeted her with a welcoming smile, easing most of her concerns. She ushered them into the kitchen, and Guy explained the situation. Sara was horrified at all Janessa had experienced.

"It's right for you to be here. Stay as long as you like." She patted Janessa's arm. "But I know you're tired after such an ordeal so I'll show you to your room. We'll talk more in the morning. Guy, will you help me with the girls?"

She led them down the hall to a dark bedroom.

"I hope you don't mind sleeping in the same room with the twins," she whispered to Janessa as Guy slipped past her into the room and moved one of the five-year-old girls to her sister's bed. He gently tucked them in together. "We don't have a spare bedroom, and Guy always takes the couch. I'm sure you'll be much more comfortable in here."

"Yeah, the couch can get a little lumpy," he added with a wink. "Maybe if it wasn't stuffed with toys—"

Janessa listened as Guy teased his sister in the same way he used to tease her when she was a teen.

She turned to Sara. "I'm really sorry to intrude. This isn't fair to you. I could stay at my apartment—"

"No!" Both Sara and Guy answered at the same time.

Sara gently squeezed Janessa's arm. "It's no imposition. When I said it's right for you to be here, I meant it. I'm just glad we can help you in your time of need. Besides, with Alex gone on a business trip, I'm happy for the distraction. The girls miss their daddy so much when he travels. So I want you to stay as long as you can." With that Sara said good night, checked on the girls one last time then backed out of the room, leaving Guy and Janessa staring at each other awkwardly.

"She really doesn't mind having you here," he confirmed, "and you'll be safe. This is a world away from anything artistic, unless you want to count color by numbers and fingerpaint."

"Do you spend a lot of time here?" she whispered.

"It's my home away from home."

Janessa wondered if he'd spent time here after Beth had broken up with him ten years ago and figured he probably had. Sara seemed so kind that she would have been a good support for Guy when he was hurting the most.

"Thank you for helping me tonight. I was so scared until you came along."

Guy grasped her shoulders firmly, looking into her eyes. "You're safe now. God won't let anything happen to you, and neither will I."

Before Janessa could murmur another word of thanks Guy leaned forward and pressed a kiss to her forehead. She winced when his lips pressed the bruised spot where she'd smacked the parked car.

"That hurt, didn't it?"

She nodded, and his lips sought to press a second kiss

to her cheek, just missing the corner of her mouth. Her pulse quickened, and she silently chastised herself for getting nervous. He was trying to comfort her as a big brother, and he would have done the same for Sara. But when his lips briefly, yet deliberately, touched hers in a third kiss she had to wonder if she was right. Did he kiss her because he felt sorry for her, or was it a mistake? Could he possibly feel anything for her? She didn't want to be humiliated again so she didn't dare respond to him.

"Good night, Janessa," he whispered before closing the door and leaving her alone with her unasked questions.

❧

Guy wasn't surprised to find his sister waiting for him in the hallway, and he could tell a dozen questions waited on the tip of her tongue. He shook his head and pointed toward the living room. He didn't want Janessa to overhear anything he said to Sara because he was certain she would be the center of their discussion.

"Tell me all about her and how you met!" Sara demanded as soon as she stepped into the family room. Her eyes sparkled with enthusiasm, and her lips twitched with curiosity. Guy knew he wouldn't get a minute's sleep until he answered every last question.

"Do you remember my mentor Walter Richards? Janessa is his granddaughter, and she's ended up in a little trouble."

He could see his vague answer only whetted his sister's appetite.

"And? You have to tell me more, Guy! I haven't seen you look at another woman since Beth, and you were never so protective of anyone—not even me. What does Janessa mean to you?"

Guy wasn't sure how to answer her question because he

hadn't allowed himself to look too closely at his feelings. Janessa was no longer the young girl he remembered, and he was attracted to her. Yet he wouldn't risk hurting her because his own feelings were uncertain. She was continually in his thoughts—to the point that he even started painting again. Where Beth had once been the subject on his canvas, Janessa had taken her place. What did this mean? Was he taking his responsibility to Walter too far? His mentor asked him to protect her, not fall in love with her. He wanted to believe his battered heart was capable of such emotion again.

"Janessa is a friend, and I want to help her. Maybe she'll become more than a friend if I handle this right," Guy answered, choosing his words carefully. "She's always been special to me, even when she was sixteen."

"And now she's older, Guy, and so are you. Many years have passed since Beth hurt you. Finally you're moving on. I can see you care about Janessa, and she seems wonderful. Trust God to guide you. Don't be afraid to share your heart again."

That's exactly what he feared, Guy realized. He wasn't sure if he could allow someone so close again and risk being hurt. And what if he wasn't capable of giving love to the degree he once had? He would only hurt Janessa or any woman who tried to get close. Seeing Beth at the benefit had brought all his old wounds to the foreground. Even now Beth didn't realize how he'd agonized over her defection—she'd walked away from him and from her promises and values. Guy didn't think he'd ever be the same after she hurt him—and he wasn't. God had guided him each day, but he was different.

"I can't make any promises except to keep her safe," Guy told his sister, his expression grim. "But I want to explore the feelings I have for her."

"For now that's enough, Guy. Don't force anything, and don't push it away. God will show you in good time."

❧

Janessa awoke to giggles and two pairs of wide blue eyes staring down at her. While both girls shared their mother's eyes, one twin had sandy blond hair like Sara; the other had light blond hair, so fair it was almost white.

"Good morning. Mommy said we couldn't wake you up—but now you're awake, and we didn't do it," the twin who resembled Sara said. "I'm Anna, and this is my sister, Jaena. I'm the older one, but she's a little taller. Did you know we're fra—fralernal twins?"

Janessa blinked, trying to hold back a smile at Anna's whirlwind introduction. "Did you know I'm Janessa? I don't even have a sister—fraternal or otherwise." Both girls looked at her solemnly. "Whose bed am I sleeping in?"

"Mine," the pale blond twin, Jaena, said shyly.

Janessa gave her a warm smile. "Thank you very much for sharing with me. I slept so well you probably thought I was going to sleep all day."

"Are you Uncle Guy's girlfriend? Mommy said Uncle Guy needs a girlfriend who can be his wife later."

Janessa stared at the little girl, uncertain how to answer. She'd love to say she was Guy's girlfriend, but they hadn't discussed such things—there were the kisses though. The wonderful kisses made her knees tremble and her heart take flight. What would the girls say to that?

She looked around the room that was stuffed with dolls, dress-up clothes, books, big toys, little toys, lots of furniture—everything but a clock. "What time is it?" she asked, hoping the girls would forget the inquisition.

A puzzled frown puckered both little faces. "I think it's nine o'clock. Or maybe it's two thirty. I don't know," Anna said with a shrug of her thin shoulders.

If it was either time Janessa had slept too late! She threw back the covers and jumped out of bed. Her head began spinning with the sudden movement.

"You have a purple lump on your head. Does it hurt?" Anna asked.

Jaena stared, as well. "Anna once hit me in the head with her cup. Apple juice got in my hair, and I had a purple lump just like yours. What happened to you?"

Janessa reached up and gingerly fingered the lump. It felt ghastly, and she was sure it was horrible to look at if the girls' interest was any indication. "I bumped a car with my head."

"Were you in a car accident?"

Janessa shook her head then regretted the movement as everything began to spin again. "No, I was running—"

"My daddy says you should never run in the street cuz you can get hit by a car," Anna said solemnly.

"Well, he's right. Now, if you'll show me where I can find the bathroom. . ."

⁂

Janessa tried to ignore the mirror while she did what she could to freshen up. Her forehead was purple and sore, and no amount of makeup would hide it so she gave up. She was thankful she'd insisted on getting a change of clothes at her apartment last night before Guy drove her to Sara's. She still felt a little awkward about imposing on his family; but his sister had been so welcoming, and the girls were gracious to share their room with a complete stranger. She needed to find a way to make it up to them.

Once she accepted she could do nothing more with her appearance, Janessa left the bathroom and went in search of

Guy. She wasn't usually interested in her looks, but deep in her heart lay an unfulfilled desire to please Guy—to get his attention and his admiration. If his kisses were any indication, maybe he was interested.

She found Guy and Sara sitting in the kitchen. Sara wore a simple blue skirt and white blouse, reminding Janessa it was Sunday. She normally would go to church and then to work after the service.

"Good morning," she murmured, drawing their attention. "I hope I'm not keeping you from going to church. May I help with anything?"

Sara gave Janessa a sweet smile, her eyes sparkling with humor. "No, you're not keeping us from going to church. The girls and I just got back. Don't look so horrified! You needed the sleep. How is your head feeling?"

Janessa's gaze darted around the room in search of a clock. The digital numbers on the stove read eleven thirty! "Oh, no! I can't believe I slept this late. I feel so rude." Her cheeks grew warm, and the room seemed to tilt at an odd angle. She didn't protest when she felt strong hands grip her shoulders and tug her toward a chair.

"Are you okay?" Guy asked. His face was inches from hers as he peered at her in concern. "Don't you think you should have your head examined?"

If he hadn't looked so serious she would have thought he was teasing. "I'm fine, Guy. I was a little dizzy, but I'm okay now. Do you think you can take me to the museum? I need to go to work."

Guy's concern turned into a frown of disapproval. "It's Sunday, Janessa. You need a day of rest, especially after what happened last night. You shouldn't work so hard."

She wasn't going to argue with him in front of his sister.

He knew perfectly well how important her work was to her because they'd discussed it before. Her work came first in her life, after the Lord of course, and it was fulfilling. She poured all she had into it, and without her work she wouldn't know what to do with herself.

"I need to make sure the Caravaggio is still there. If Mrs. Pembroke comes in to pick up her painting, I want to talk to her." She didn't voice her concerns that Ted might not tell the truth to the dear lady. He had promised to turn *The Maiden* over to Mrs. Pembroke along with the new copy of the yellow flowers, but she was suspicious of him—especially after the phone conversation she'd overheard. At the very least Janessa needed to be certain Mrs. Pembroke understood what had happened to her original painting.

❧

After a short battle of wills Guy finally gave in to Janessa's arguments, insisting he would take her to the museum as long as she allowed him to stay. That was fine with her; Janessa's foolish heart was more than happy to agree with his demand.

He drove silently through Rochester, heading toward the museum. Janessa stole small glances at his profile. It was impossible for her to be near him and not want to stare—even after all these years. She should have outgrown the silly crush long ago, but she hadn't. She still loved him.

"I can't talk you out of going in to work, can I? We could go shopping or to a movie, maybe a walk through the park? You aren't still dizzy, are you?" he asked, catching her in the act of staring at him.

Janessa looked away quickly but not before she noticed the twinkle of amusement in his eyes. Great. He was laughing at her. "No! I'm fine. I need to go in," she answered more crossly than she intended. She wondered what Guy would be doing if he weren't stuck babysitting her. He would probably have gone to church with his sister and would be playing with his nieces right now. Would they ask him about his new "girlfriend"?

"Look—I appreciate your help, but you don't have to watch over me. I can take care of myself. I could have called a cab or ridden a bus across town. I feel as if I'm taking up too much of your time."

Guy shook his head. "I don't think you understand. I'm not offering my time because I feel sorry for you. Yes, someone attacked you in the parking lot. You have a knot on your forehead the size of my fist—okay, that was a slight exaggeration," he amended when she gave him a sharp look. "I'm offering my time because I want to be with you. And if you didn't need my help right now, I would look for excuses to spend time with you."

Janessa stared at him, hoping she had heard correctly. When she didn't answer he continued, "I don't think you're taking this seriously enough. You could be in real danger."

"Because of the Caravaggio." Janessa sighed. It was strange that such a beautiful painting could cause so much trouble.

"I don't want to alarm you, but I plan to spend today and every day with you—and you can't chase me away."

Janessa opened her mouth to protest that she didn't want to cause him any more hassles, but he gave her a look of warning that allowed no argument.

"What about Beth?"

Guy raised his brows. "What about her?"

"I thought you would want to see her after being apart for so long. I'm sure she has plenty to share with you. I've never seen anyone so happy to be with another person as when she saw you in the museum." Janessa tried to remove any emotion from her voice so she sounded like a concerned friend, but with each word she felt more and more depressed. She didn't want to send him away to be with Beth, but she wouldn't selfishly keep him if he wanted to be somewhere else.

Guy's grip tightened on the steering wheel. "Let's get this straight. I'm staying with you." He reached over and switched on the radio, concluding the discussion.

Janessa sat back in her seat, hoping she hadn't made him angry. His tension caused her to question his sense of obligation toward her. She tried to release him from that duty. If he wanted to be stubborn, then there was no sense being angry about it!

The news broadcast broke into Janessa's thoughts.

*"This just in—authorities in Rochester have reported a break-in at the Museum of Fine Art."*

Janessa gasped at the radio announcement. Guy reached for the dial and turned up the volume.

*"Offices were ransacked, but the main gallery remained untouched. It's unclear what the burglar was after because nothing was stolen or vandalized, according to the museum's curator, Ted Devroe—"*

Janessa didn't have to tell Guy to drive faster. She had to get to the museum to make sure the Caravaggio was still there. In her heart she felt a sense of dread and prayed she wouldn't somehow be connected to the break-in.

❧

The front lawn of the museum was covered with police, reporters, and curious spectators when they arrived. They wove their way through the crowd until Janessa was able to reach Ted. He looked haggard and frustrated, and she felt a jolt of pity for him. He was responsible for so much, and because of the break-in he wouldn't look good to the general public, not to mention the private contributors.

Janessa slipped to his side and touched his arm—not only to let him know she was there but also to help in any way she could.

"Did the security system malfunction, or was it an inside job?" a reporter asked, shoving her microphone in Ted's face. Before he could answer, a policeman intervened.

"They're finished checking for prints inside. Let's continue the questioning away from the media. It's like a circus out here!"

With a sigh Ted turned to Janessa. "It's about time you got here! I could have used your help. Where were you? And why are you with him?" His gaze traveled past her to Guy, and Janessa knew she didn't have the right answer to his question— one that would please him, at any rate. With a scowl Ted's gaze returned to her.

"You look terrible! Your head—what happened?"

"It's a long story." She didn't want to explain in front of the media and museum patrons that she had been attacked in the parking lot. The police already knew and would handle it, as they promised.

"What about the Caravaggio?" she whispered as they moved toward the door. "I heard your office was ransacked. What about the painting?"

Ted stopped suddenly, and she nearly bumped into him. "It was stolen, Janessa. It's gone," he whispered, his voice flat.

She gaped at him in horror. "What did the police say when you told them? We had no idea if it was an original or what it might be worth. What are you going to tell—"

Ted suddenly gripped her arm, and she winced at the pain. "It hasn't been reported. And it *won't* be reported. Do you understand?" he growled softly.

Janessa barely nodded, noticing that Mrs. Pembroke was nearby and could have been within earshot. Her shrewd gaze pinned Janessa, and she felt an uncomfortable jolt. Was Mrs. Pembroke there because she was worried about her painting? Until this mess was resolved, Ted would have to find a way to appease the woman.

"I'm glad you're willing to work with me on this, Janessa. This could become a sticky situation, and we have to handle it with the greatest caution." His gaze took in both her and Guy who wasn't far behind her. Guy seemed distracted by the people trying to crowd into the art museum, but she didn't doubt he'd heard every word Ted spoke.

As far as she was concerned the situation was already sticky and dangerous. She'd been threatened in the parking lot the night before the museum was robbed. Assuredly the police would have more questions for her. She couldn't understand why Ted insisted on complete secrecy. This went way beyond preserving his reputation, and every nerve in Janessa's body tingled with suspicion.

Tension radiated through Ted's fingertips into her arm. "Do you hear me, Janessa? We need to work together."

"I'll work with you as long as you're not the thief," she retorted, gaining a scowl from both Ted and Guy.

# seven

"I don't think you should be so willing to comply with Ted Devroe," Guy insisted once they were out of earshot of Ted and the police. "You need to do what the police say."

"I *am* doing what the police said. Besides, Ted is my boss, Guy. He makes the decisions concerning this museum and any project I work on. If I fight him, I lose my job. If I work with him, I might be able to learn more about what's going on around here."

Guy shoved his hand through his hair in frustration. "That's just it. I don't want you snooping around in these matters. You've already seen it can become dangerous. Tell the police all you know, and then stay out of it. They told you to take a few days off anyway, just to be safe."

"I can't, Guy. This is more than a paycheck to me. I can't risk losing my position by taking unnecessary time away." If she lost her job she would lose the one thing that made her feel valuable. Her grandfather may not approve of her work, but many people did. They respected her. Even in her church she was known for her artistic expertise. Without it she was afraid she would become a nobody people looked through but never saw.

The police made the decision on whether to stay or not. They needed more time to study the crime scene and didn't want the public tromping through the corridors. So the museum was closed for the day and everyone was sent away.

When Janessa declined Guy's offer to go back to his sister's, he insisted on taking her home. She didn't want to impose any more than she already had. And in the quiet of her apartment she could think about the strange occurrences and maybe find a missing clue she had overlooked. She hadn't thought Guy would stay with her.

"We're not going over this again, Janessa. I'm spending the day with you," Guy said as he climbed the stairs to her apartment. "I want to be with you."

"But my apartment is safe. Nobody knows where I live—not even Ted, unless he looks at my employee file at the museum. I really don't think you should waste your day on me." She didn't add that she would feel awkward having him in her home and knew they couldn't spend the day there.

Guy stopped on the landing outside her door and waited for her to hand him the key. "Again we need to get a few things straight. Number one, *no one* is completely anonymous these days. With the Internet, phone directories, even private investigators, it would be very easy—too easy—to find you. Besides, I promised your—" He stopped.

Janessa located her key and looked up at Guy. He was frowning. "You promised what?"

It took a moment for him to answer, and Janessa knew he'd changed what he was going to say.

"I promised to spend the day with you. You can't talk me out of it, no matter how stubborn you get. I really do like spending time with you, Nessa. I always have."

*Nessa.* No one called her that anymore, but it sounded right coming from him. When he leaned forward and pressed his lips softly against her bruised forehead she wanted to cry out in agony—not from pain, but from the well of feelings she was trying to keep buried.

Guy took the key from her limp fingers and fitted it into

the door. With a little effort he managed to work the lock. "Is it always this difficult to unlock?"

Janessa shrugged. "Always." But it didn't bother her because she was used to the idiosyncrasies of her apartment.

Guy followed her into the apartment. She looked around self-consciously, wondering what he thought of her home. When they'd stopped by the night before to pick up a few necessities, he'd waited in the darkened entryway. Today he followed her into the living room.

"This is really nice—bright light perfect for painting. Comfortable and homey. It's a lot bigger than my apartment."

Janessa didn't know how to answer his compliment. She felt nervous having him see her apartment. "Would you like something to drink or eat? It's been awhile since breakfast. I could fix you something—"

"I'm fine." He walked over to the bookcase that held her eclectic collection. She had numerous volumes of classic literature, poetry, modern Christian fiction, and study books of Renaissance art. And propped in front of the books were snapshots of her friends and family.

"Do you miss your parents?" he asked.

Janessa nodded. "I don't always know where they are. Last I knew they were in the Mediterranean, but I'm sure they've moved on to a new assignment. I'm hoping they'll come back in June for a few weeks."

"But you have your friends." He held up a snapshot of her and Rosy. At that time Rosy's hair was long, curly, and blond. They could have passed for sisters. "No boyfriend?" he added casually.

He had to ask after the way she'd responded to his kiss at the benefit? Couldn't he see she'd never had room for a boyfriend when she carried his image so close to her heart?

She had prayed God would help her get over Guy, but it hadn't happened. "Are you collecting data or asking for personal reasons?" she bantered.

Guy turned to her, his gaze warm and intense, making nervous butterflies roil in her stomach. "Definitely personal reasons," he answered with all seriousness. With two long strides he crossed to stand near Janessa. She felt mesmerized by the deep blue of his eyes as he gazed at her.

Janessa wanted to ask him about his reasons and whether she played a part in them. Was Beth still in the picture, too? But her lips couldn't form the words with Guy standing so close. Just when she thought he might kiss her as he had before, they were interrupted by the shrill ring of the phone.

"I should get that," she murmured while it rang a second then third time.

As she picked up the phone she noticed the blinking light on her answering machine. "Hello?"

"Darling! Are you well? I haven't heard your precious voice for so long!"

"Mom!"

"Are you coming down with a cold or something? Your voice sounds different."

Janessa glanced at Guy and blushed as though he were able to hear her mom's question. "Uh, no, I'm fine. I have a friend over, but I think we'll be leaving soon. You caught me just in time." It was definitely in her best interest to leave before her imagination ran away with her and she convinced herself Guy loved her as much as she loved him! "Did you need me to do something for you, Mom? Where are you?"

"No. You already do too much as it is—helping us on the home front and all. I just wanted to let you know we'll be in New York in the next few weeks. This assignment is nearly finished, and we'll have a little time before the next one begins. How is everything with you?"

Janessa considered telling her mom about the Caravaggio painting and the strange events at the museum but decided against it. Her mom would only worry, and she couldn't do anything. "I'm busy as always. Ted gives me very little space to breathe in, but it's all right because you know how I enjoy my work." Janessa paused, turning her back on Guy. "Mom, Guy is here. You remember him?"

"Guy Langly?"

"Mm-hmm." She waited to hear her mother's reaction. Her affection for Guy was no secret to her parents. They had met him numerous times when Janessa had lived with her grandfather and Guy was there to work. Even though her grandfather had been stiff and formal with her parents, they hadn't hesitated to visit as much as their travel schedule would allow.

"He was a wonderful man when I met him, and I hope nothing has changed," her mom said. "God is in the business of making dreams come true."

"I'm trusting Him for this, Mom, with no other expectations."

"All right, darling. Your father gives you his love. We'll see you soon!"

As Janessa disconnected the line she again noticed the flashing light indicating a message. She pressed the button, wondering if Rosy had called.

A stranger's voice filled the quiet of her apartment.

"I already warned you. If you know where the painting is, you better return it to the museum. Leave it inside the back door in a brown wrapper. I'd hate to come looking for it myself. You would hate that, as well."

Janessa started when Guy stepped close to her. Her heart

pounded furiously in her chest, and her mind raced with what she should do. She recognized the man's voice. It was the same man who had threatened her in the parking lot. How had he gotten her home phone number? Surely he didn't know her name or her address! Then she remembered Guy had told her how easy it was to find personal information. She wasn't safe. Even though she didn't know where the painting was, she was in danger.

"I don't have it, Guy! I don't know where the painting is, but this person seems to think I do. What am I supposed to do? I don't have the foggiest idea how to handle this."

Guy turned her to face him and wrapped his arms around her. His embrace had a soothing effect. Gradually her breathing quieted, and her heart slowed its frantic beating.

"God will protect you, Janessa, and I'm here for you. You don't have to handle this alone."

"What should I do?"

"What are the chances Ted Devroe is still at the museum?"

"Pretty good. This break-in won't cast him in a positive light, and I'm sure he'll work until things look better for him."

"Can you get into the museum without disturbing him?"

Slowly Janessa nodded, wondering what Guy was getting at. Did he plan to spy on Ted Devroe? If Ted caught them in the museum he would ask more questions, and Janessa didn't know what explanations she could give. She didn't like this cloak-and-dagger business, sneaking around while a painting was missing and someone suspected her of stealing it. But until the painting was found she was in danger.

"Go pack more clothes for several days while I make a phone call," Guy ordered. Janessa didn't waste any time arguing. Staying at his sister's was an imposition, but the alternative of staying alone was a terrifying prospect.

❧

"I can see now your hunch was right. She is in danger." Guy clenched his cell phone in a grip that threatened to crush it. Putting his suspicions into words made his heart pound with fear, and he had to remind himself that God would protect her. No matter how weak or ineffectual he was, God would never fail.

"What's happened?" Walter demanded. His tone was gruff with suspicion, and Guy had the feeling Walter wanted to pin the blame on him.

"She was threatened in the museum parking lot. A man warned her to stay away from a painting she discovered—a Caravaggio she believes is authentic."

When Walter sucked in his breath at the mention of the baroque painter, Guy knew he had the older man's undivided attention. "And when she ran away from the punk, she was injured, but she's fine now—and the police have been notified."

"Do you think it's the same person who broke into the museum?"

"I believe the two are connected. What makes me certain is Janessa received a message on her answering machine at home. She says it was the same person who threatened her before. He warned her to return the missing painting to the museum."

The line was quiet as Walter apparently assimilated this new information.

"They know where she lives, and they're pinning the blame on her. You have to stick with her twenty-four hours a day. I don't care how you do it; just don't tell her I've insisted. If they know where she lives, then they will also know when you leave her alone. She can't be alone!"

"Do you really think they'd hurt her?" Guy asked. Janessa

could continue staying at his sister's home if there wasn't a chance the danger would follow her. No way would he put Sara and the twins at risk. Protecting Janessa was a full-time job in itself. He couldn't imagine trying to protect Sara's family, as well, from someone he couldn't identify.

"If they're desperate, they will try anything to get that painting," Walter answered grimly.

"It would be easier to protect her if I knew who *they* were," Guy muttered. He had his own suspicions—with Ted Devroe at the top of his list. Yet it didn't make sense why he would stage a break-in at the museum—unless he was trying to divert suspicion away from himself and onto an unknown criminal. "She thinks you're involved, too. She heard you talking to Devroe about the painting. What are you doing, Walter? Are you involved? What aren't you telling me?"

"I'll make a few discreet inquiries, but don't expect any answers soon. Just keep Janessa away from Devroe. Whether he's involved or not, I don't want him manipulating her," Walter warned him.

"You're not answering my questions!"

"Keep her safe from everyone—keep the Pembrokes away, Devroe, this nutcase, and anyone else who might try to hurt her. Stay with her night and day."

Guy drew in his breath. "Aside from her safety, Walter, your suggestion isn't appropriate. I can't stay with her *night* and day. It wouldn't be right."

"Then make it right! Marry the girl, or do whatever you have to do!" Walter bellowed into the phone. "Any fool could see she's loved you for years. If you had an ounce of common sense, you would have seen it for yourself and done something long before now."

Guy was speechless. Surely Walter wasn't serious. Marry

Janessa? "You must be joking—"

"I never joke about my granddaughter!" Walter barked then hung up.

Guy stared at his phone in disbelief, expecting it to ring. When he answered it Walter would tell him he was only teasing. Yet the phone remained silent, and as the seconds stretched into minutes Guy's indignation rose. How dare Walter suggest such a preposterous thing! Had he done it to avoid difficult questions? Guy had agreed to watch over Janessa and make sure she stayed out of harm's way. He never imagined Walter would want them to marry just to protect her. Guy knew he owed Walter many favors, but he wouldn't go so far as to force his granddaughter on Guy. Walter had no right to interfere in anyone's personal life—not Guy's and not Janessa's.

Was Walter right about Janessa's feelings? He knew she had a crush on him when she was young, and even now she blushed easily. But it was difficult to imagine the professional, independent woman in love with him. So much had changed in his life. He was no longer the popular artist but a bookstore manager and a temporary handyman in a museum. Could she still be attracted to him? She seemed willing to accept his kisses, but did that willingness extend to marriage? She was so busy trying to please everyone and prove herself that he doubted she had time to consider her own feelings.

The idea of marriage wasn't at all intimidating. In fact, he was ready to be settled in his life with someone he loved. Was Janessa the right person for him? If he did marry her, he could help her see how valuable she was. She wouldn't have to strive to please him or anyone else—especially her grandfather—if he became her husband. He'd make sure she was safe, not only physically but also emotionally. No one would ever hurt her or make her feel insecure again if he could help it. Yet he knew he was skirting the real issues for getting married. Emotional support and protection weren't viable reasons to commit his life to someone. Love needed to be the foundation in a Christian marriage. Could he love Janessa?

"I can't believe I'm actually thinking about this," he murmured.

Janessa stepped onto the landing outside her apartment door where Guy was waiting for her. A heavy bag was slung over her shoulder. When Guy tried to help her with it, she protested.

"I can carry it. It's my stuff, after all."

"Will you stop fighting me? I want to be with you and help carry the load. Just let me, okay? You don't owe me for any of this." When he reached for the bag a second time she let him take it.

"I'm really thankful to have you with me, Guy. I've missed you these last years. I've had to work hard and am not used to relying on anyone else but myself."

"Well, consider it a vacation when you're with me. That's what friends are for."

Janessa shook her head. "I really meant it when I said I've missed you. It's hard for me to express exactly how much. I'm afraid I'll wake up and find you gone." Her eyes misted, and she turned her head quickly; but Guy saw the vulnerable look she tried to hide.

"I'm here now, and I'm not going anywhere. You can count on me." He gently tipped her chin up so she was forced to look at him. As he stared into her eyes, he realized he was growing more and more serious about Walter's suggestion. Janessa could very well become his bride—his true love. But he couldn't put words to his thoughts until he was sure of himself.

"Are you ready to go?" he said instead.

Janessa nodded. "Yes, I have enough clothes for several days, but where are we going?"

"I have no idea," he admitted. "Maybe we should start with lunch and go from there."

# eight

They went to Janessa's favorite pizza place near the museum. As she slid into the booth she prayed she wouldn't make a fool of herself by spilling soda all over Guy again. She felt nervous, but she wasn't sure why. Something had changed. He seemed more introspective since his phone conversation—and more attentive. Whom had he called? Beth? If he had talked with Beth and wanted to be with her, surely he wouldn't act so conscientious now—or would he?

"You don't have to babysit me," Janessa muttered as she fiddled with her soda straw. She made the offer, but she hoped he wanted to stay with her. It was difficult for her to believe he wasn't there out of obligation.

"Is there someone you'd rather be with? Someone you're dating maybe?" Guy responded.

Janessa hadn't expected this question. She looked up to find him studying her with his intense blue eyes. "No, I don't have time to date. My work is very involved. Please don't look at me like that. I'm not the only person on earth who doesn't date."

Guy's lips turned up in amusement, but he apparently wasn't ready to give up the subject. "Does Rosy date? She works with you, right?"

How could Janessa explain? Sure, Rosy dated. Most men developed a drooling problem when they were around the stunning, vivacious charmer. One look at her and all men forgot Janessa existed. Even if they noticed her, she wasn't interested in them. Her foolish heart refused to give up on

Guy, but she wasn't about to admit that to him—at least not yet. "You've seen Rosy. She dates all the time because she's in the market for a husband."

"And you're not?" He seemed particularly interested in her answer as he leaned forward.

"Have you taken a good look at me lately, Guy? What man is going to choose me over Rosy? I know I'm not a great catch, but I'm okay with it. I accept the way things are."

Unexpectedly Guy reached across the table and brushed his finger slowly down her cheek. Warmth filled her face at his touch, and she had difficulty meeting his gaze.

"You have a skewed picture of yourself. All you care about is your work, and it's making you sick." When she tried to protest, he shook his head. "I've seen the bottle of medicine on your desk. You stress yourself out to please others."

"But my work is important. It's all I have going for me."

"I don't know exactly what you see in the mirror, but when I look at you I see someone warm, kind, and beautiful. I see someone who works too hard to please others but is a blessing to everyone who knows her. When I look at you, Janessa, I see loveliness."

His words made a lump form in Janessa's throat, and it was difficult for her to breathe around it. No one aside from her parents had ever said she was lovely. "Thanks, Guy," she whispered.

She glanced past him, and her gaze connected with that of a strange man sitting a few tables away. She wouldn't have thought anything of it except he was frowning at her. She didn't notice anything striking about him; he had dark hair, light eyes, and a thin build. He seemed to be in his forties. When his lip curled in derision, Janessa nervously broke the gaze.

"What is it?" Guy questioned.

"Don't turn around, but someone is staring at me. He might be the man who threatened me," she whispered. When her hands began to tremble, she tucked them in her lap. "Is it possible he's following me?"

Despite her caution Guy turned in his seat. The man was no longer looking at Janessa but had stuck his head behind a menu so Guy couldn't see his face. Janessa knew what he looked like, and every instinct told her this was the man who wanted the Caravaggio from her. He knew where she lived. He was following her. What could she do to escape? She didn't have the painting, and even if she did she certainly wouldn't give it to a thief!

"Should I go talk to him? We can get this out in the open here and now."

Frantically Janessa shook her head. "No, Guy! He could be dangerous. I don't want you to have anything to do with him. Please, let's go!" When she pulled urgently on his hand, he slid from the booth. She stepped to his side, and he wrapped his arm around her shoulders in a protective gesture.

"He's going to follow us," Guy murmured in Janessa's ear. "But we're going to lose him." He took the heavy overnight bag that held her clothes and draped it over his shoulder. He then led Janessa casually out the front door so the man watching them wouldn't be suspicious of their sudden departure. To the world it appeared they were on a casual date, but Janessa's pounding heart knew the truth.

Once outside Guy quickened his pace. Janessa wanted to look back to see if the man had followed them, but she didn't dare. They hurried a few yards down the street then ducked into a printer's shop.

"Excuse me. You have a back door?" Guy asked the young man behind the counter.

"Straight back—you can't miss it," the clerk answered, giving them a puzzled look.

"Thanks. We owe you one." Guy tugged on Janessa's hand, and they darted through the shop to the rear door leading into the alley. He didn't stop to look around but hurried down the dark passage to the street.

"Now where?" Janessa said, gasping. Guy hadn't slowed long enough to allow either of them to catch their breath. She glanced over her shoulder, expecting to see the strange man, but no one followed them.

"To the museum. You said Ted is probably there. Let's see if we can snoop around without raising his suspicion."

Janessa gave him a doubtful look. She wasn't sure she liked going to the museum under false pretenses—yet were they false? Normally she'd be there, working long into the night. What did it matter that she was going there for other purposes? If they could find a clue about the Caravaggio, it would help both her and Ted.

"It's okay, Janessa," Guy assured her. "You and I have permission to be on the premises, and we won't do anything wrong. I just want to take a look around. Maybe we'll find something before Ted has a chance to hide it."

They hurried to the museum, taking back streets to avoid being seen. Rather than marching up to the front entrance they approached the side door Janessa always used. She pulled her security card from her purse and punched in the required code. A low buzz sounded before the lock clicked, allowing them entry.

"So far so good," she muttered, adding a silent prayer that God would keep them safe. Her heart beat a rapid staccato, and she was sure Guy could hear it. After the recent threats against her she felt someone was watching her every move, waiting to catch her off guard.

Guy wrenched the door open and stepped inside, looking in all directions before allowing her to follow. When he motioned for her she crept after him, thankful for the silent rubber soles on her shoes.

She was surprised when he led her straight toward Ted's office. He crept up to the door that stood partially open. They could hear Ted inside, muttering to himself.

Janessa squeezed Guy's hand in protest. She didn't dare speak in case Ted heard them and demanded to know why they were spying on him. Guy turned and gave her a conspiratorial wink before easing closer to the doorway. The phone inside the office rang, startling Janessa so much she almost cried out.

"Devroe here," Ted barked into the phone. Janessa had heard his tone before and knew it meant he was displeased.

"Yeah, I wasn't surprised with the media response. No, the painting is safe. I've got it hidden here, but I don't like it. I don't care for these games at all. Why don't you come take it off my hands?"

Guy stiffened, and Janessa had a feeling he was just as suspicious of Ted as she was. Ted was practically admitting he'd stolen the painting—after he assured her it was gone. Was he talking with her grandfather again?

As Ted hung up the phone with a clatter Guy eased away from the door. Apparently he'd heard enough. Janessa certainly had, and she felt sickened by it. She couldn't believe Ted would take the painting. He'd promised to handle it in his own way, and though Janessa had felt suspicious at the time, she'd still hoped he was trustworthy. This proved he was a thief.

"Let's find the painting, Guy! We have to save Mrs. Pembroke's masterpiece before Ted sells it to the highest bidder." Janessa strode toward her workroom with Guy hurrying after her. She didn't know where to start looking for the painting in a museum full of artwork. Ted could have hidden it anywhere. Yet she had a feeling it wouldn't be where the public could spot it. He wouldn't risk having his actions filmed by security cameras or by allowing anyone else to see a painting that supposedly didn't exist. Few people knew about it, and Ted would want to keep it that way.

Janessa unlocked her workroom and stepped inside. Rather than switching on the bright overhead lights she fumbled toward her desk and turned on the tabletop lamp. Its soft light cast shadows across the room. She scanned the room, hoping Ted had tucked the painting in with her things, though it was unlikely.

"Where is the least obvious hiding place?" she questioned, looking around the room that appeared untouched since she'd last left it. She wished Rosy were there to help solve the mystery. She had a knack for puzzles.

"Or, rather, where is the *most* obvious hiding place?" Guy countered. "Sometimes we look too hard when it's right under our noses." He glanced around. "Where do you keep extra supplies? Ted won't pick a place where the painting would be easily damaged so the maintenance rooms are out."

"And the administration offices get a lot of traffic. I could picture him hanging the painting on one of the office walls, but he could risk damaging it. Let's look in the supply room first."

Janessa led the way to a small room, not much bigger than a closet, that held various odds and ends to repair canvases. It smelled musty. She stepped into the darkness, knowing the way around the room without light. But she was relieved when Guy switched on the bare bulb that hung in the center of the room. She didn't care so much for the darkness anymore.

"See anything?" she whispered.

Nothing appeared out of order. She saw no place to hide a painting on the neat, organized shelves. She gave a sigh of disappointment.

"We could try the admin offices. Maybe you're right, and Ted hung the painting over a secretary's computer. Most people wouldn't question having artwork in the offices of a museum."

Janessa shook her head. She didn't want to go back to that end of the museum and risk Ted knowing of their presence. "Too chancy. Let's go back to my workroom."

Guy looked as disappointed as she felt. "Tomorrow I'll poke around the administration offices. They won't think anything of my offering to make repairs. Maybe I'll come across something promising."

"And Ted might make a slip. He often tells me details of different business dealings even though it's none of my concern."

Guy gave her a sharp look. "You're close to him, aren't you?"

"Not as close as he'd like." Janessa gave a casual shrug. "Ted isn't interested in me. He pretends, thinking his attention will make me work harder. I know better."

"Don't be so sure. I've seen how he looks at you—like a boy with his face pressed to the pet shop window."

Guy's words made Janessa feel uneasy. She didn't want Ted to be interested in her, and she never took him seriously. But in light of their new discoveries having Ted's attention made her even more uncomfortable—and scared.

"Let's get out of here, Janessa. We need to make plans."

"What sort of plans?" she asked distractedly, taking one last look around her workroom. Her gaze fell to the stack of canvases propped against the wall, awaiting restoration.

"You obviously can't stay home alone tonight."

"I won't stay at your sister's house again. I don't want

her or the girls getting pulled into my troubles. I'm sure you understand, Guy. There has to be another way," she murmured as she crossed the room to the neglected paintings. They represented hours of work, and she wished she could turn away from them.

"I agree you shouldn't stay with Sara in case the weirdo who's following you decides to add my sister to his list."

Janessa stiffened at his choice of words but didn't comment. It was true a stranger who knew far too much about her was watching her. She'd never willingly bring Sara or anyone else into her problems. Too bad she couldn't get lost in her work and forget about this nightmare. So many projects were waiting for her. She thumbed through the canvases from different eras, each telling its own story from a time long past.

"So the way I see it, you don't have many options. Rosy is out of town so you can't stay with her. You can't be alone in your apartment. That leaves your grandfather."

"No! He'd never have me. He'd say I brought this mess upon myself. Besides, I know he's involved."

Guy nodded as though he'd expected her protest. "You can spend the night in a hotel, but I don't think that's a good idea either since someone was following you."

Janessa noticed a canvas pressed between the others that hadn't been there before. Had Rosy placed it there?

"And what's my third option?" she asked absently.

"You can go home with me."

Janessa looked up at Guy in shock. "How could I? It wouldn't be right," she whispered, her eyes wide as she stared at him in surprise.

"It would be if you were my wife."

❧

Guy knew he'd muddled the situation by the astounded look

on Janessa's face. He could see she was surprised, and he expected that; but her total shock wounded him. He wanted her to be flattered by his suggestion and fall into his arms. Her stony white-faced horror wasn't near what he anticipated from the girl who once adored him. Boy, had he missed the mark!

The idea of marrying Janessa had been tucked into the back of his mind ever since Walter suggested it. He had to ask himself if he considered the idea because of Walter's wishes or his own? Did he love Janessa? Did he want to spend the rest of his life with her? He couldn't possibly consider marrying her just to keep her safe and within the bounds of respectability. That wasn't enough on which to base a marriage. Yet taking Janessa as his wife felt right—almost as though God were leading him in that direction. Was this what God had in mind all the time when Guy prayed for healing of his heart?

Seconds lengthened as he returned Janessa's gaze of confusion. He wanted to take her in his arms and tell her to forget what he said if it was so troubling to her. But at the same time he didn't want her to forget it. He wanted her to consider his offer seriously.

"Maybe we should go now," she whispered, sounding strained. She strode toward the door keeping a wide space between them.

Guy didn't want to go just yet. If they talked about it maybe he could help her see that his idea wasn't so bad. The more he thought about it, the more he liked it. Why did she have to look like a scared rabbit with a big wolf at her heels? Granted, he was no fine catch these days. He had nothing to offer in the way of luxurious living, and that probably wouldn't change soon. Once Janessa's situation was secure he would quit the job as museum handyman and go back to managing the bookstore. It wasn't a glamorous life, but he had more than enough money. Had he asked Beth instead of Janessa, she would have scoffed at him.

He wanted someone to love him for himself, not what he could provide. Beth had taught him a valuable lesson on what was important in life. Plastic surgery and diamonds meant very little to him but had cost him Beth's affection when he refused to provide them. He knew Janessa was different. Rather than fur coats and champagne parties, Janessa valued her work and the admiration she gained from her clients. His proposal should have shown her he valued her, as well. But his muddled efforts only confused her.

*Love her unconditionally as I do.*

The gentle thought followed on the heels of his frustration, and he knew the Lord was right. Guy was certain Janessa's parents loved her unconditionally; but Walter never had, and Janessa was still striving to please him. With her parents so far away maybe she had forgotten what unconditional love felt like.

"Let's go to the park and talk about this," Guy murmured. When he touched her arm he felt an electric jolt shoot through his fingers and up his arm. By the startled look on Janessa's face he knew she felt it, as well.

Meekly she nodded and followed him out of the workroom into the deserted hallway. They walked softly to the outer door, being careful not to alert Ted to their presence. In the distance they heard someone whistling.

"It's only Joe," Guy murmured, remembering the other custodian who worked on the weekends. Janessa didn't seem to be listening.

As they reached the end of the hall she stopped suddenly.

"Wait! I need to go back to my workroom. I think I know where the Caravaggio is hidden!"

# nine

"Now we really need to get out of here," Guy muttered as he led Janessa around the back of the museum. She carried a large canvas tote designed for transporting artwork. He kept a firm grasp on her hand, unwilling to break contact with her for a second. He didn't like to think about the priceless painting tucked inside the rectangular tote, an obvious enticement for the stranger who had been following them. Guy wondered if Walter had had any success in learning the man's identity.

"We should take this straight to Mrs. Pembroke. It's her painting, and she deserves to know of its existence," Janessa said firmly as though she expected an argument from him.

The Pembrokes—Walter had warned him to keep Janessa away from them. "Isn't she expecting a painting with yellow flowers? This will certainly come as a shock to her." Guy calculated the quickest route to his apartment—or Walter's. He knew he couldn't take Janessa back to her home where the stalker might be waiting for her to hand over the painting.

"Guy!" Janessa tugged on his hand. "We need to go back to my apartment and get your car. Then you can take me to Mrs. Pembroke's house. She should know about her painting."

Guy didn't want to go to either destination, but he knew Janessa was determined to talk to Mrs. Pembroke. He felt as if someone was watching them from every doorway and from around each corner as they hurried the few blocks to her apartment. Once they reached Guy's car in the parking lot they were both gasping for breath. With a quick prayer of thanks for their safety, Guy helped Janessa into the car and hurried around to the driver's side.

"I don't think you should talk to Mrs. Pembroke right now."

"Why?"

*Because your grandfather warned me to keep you away from them.* He couldn't tell her that. "We have to be careful."

"I know. And that's why you'll be with me the entire time. I promise it won't take long, and maybe she'll have an idea of what we should do."

Following Janessa's directions Guy reluctantly drove to Mrs. Pembroke's house. The woman was about to receive a surprise when she learned her beloved painting was in fact a rare masterpiece. Guy agreed with Janessa that Mrs. Pembroke should have been notified from the beginning when the Caravaggio was discovered. Yet Walter was suspicious of the Pembrokes. Why? He wished he had the answers to this puzzle. Then he would know who was harassing Janessa.

"There's the house." She pointed to a colonial-style house made of red brick. Every window was dark.

"It looks as if no one's home." He hopped out of the car and hurried to the door. When no one answered his knock he returned. "All's quiet," he said with relief, glad they could postpone giving away the painting to its owner. He felt sure with a little more time the mystery would reveal itself and everything would be back to normal.

"She's probably at a committee meeting or something. Mrs. Pembroke is the busiest person I know."

Guy turned in his seat, giving Janessa a cynical smile. "Even busier than you? I doubt that." He couldn't help reaching out to tuck a stray strand of hair back behind her ear. When his fingers brushed against her cheek, Janessa sucked in a sharp breath.

"We should talk about us, Janessa."

She shook her head. "In front of Mrs. Pembroke's house? Now? I don't think we should." Again the panic returned to her voice, making Guy frown.

"Why are you running from this? Even when your grandfather pushed you about your artwork you faced him head-on and fought for what you believed in. Why run now? Is it because I completely ruined my proposal? I should have given you flowers and a candlelight dinner, but I behaved like an oaf. I'm sure the thought of marrying me must be offensive to you."

Guy didn't want to look at Janessa for fear of the rejection he might find in her gaze. He hadn't exposed himself like this in ten years, and it was an uncomfortable sensation. Yet he needed to know if the teenager who had loved him once still felt the same now that she was grown. "Please, Janessa," he whispered.

"Do you love me, Guy? Is that why you think we should get married, or is it something else? You've been gone ten years. Then you show up from out of nowhere and announce we should get married. How am I supposed to respond? My head is spinning, and my entire life feels out of control right now."

Janessa turned her gaze toward him, and he was surprised by the open vulnerability he saw there. Even while he was afraid she'd reject him he sensed she feared the same thing. He'd wanted honesty from her, and she deserved the truth, as well. He knew he wanted to love her and had always loved her as a friend. Worded like that, he didn't think she would be convinced of his sincerity. And above all she needed to know he was serious about this.

"I don't know how to answer your questions, Janessa. But I do know when I'm with you I feel complete and when we're apart something vital is missing. I think we should pray about it and consider it."

"Okay, let's pray about it," Janessa agreed. Together they bowed their heads and went before God. When they finished praying Guy felt sure in his heart that Janessa was the one for him. He also realized she needed more time.

Guy put the car in gear and slowly drove away from Mrs. Pembroke's house. Janessa sat silently beside him. He wanted to ask her what she thought but kept his questions to himself. Somehow it would all come together for them.

A few minutes later they arrived at his apartment. Guy was committed to protecting Janessa and staying with her continually as Walter suggested, but he wouldn't do anything improper. She didn't feel comfortable calling any of her friends or someone from church. He suspected she didn't want to involve anyone else in her complicated situation or answer difficult questions. So their only alternative was Walter. He knew Janessa wouldn't like it, but he wasn't about to drop her off at a hotel to fend for herself.

❧

"Why are we stopping here?" Janessa asked as she stared curiously at Guy's apartment building.

"I need a change of clothes and a few things. Come up with me. I don't want to leave you alone in the car—especially with the painting."

She followed him into his apartment but left the front door wide open. While he darted into his bedroom to pack a few clothes she wandered into the brightly lit living room. It was sparsely furnished with only a sofa to sit on. A stereo stood on the floor in the corner. It appeared he'd just moved in, but Janessa knew better. When she caught sight of the easel near the window she knew why Guy didn't bother with a television or computer. No canvas was propped up on the easel, but his paint case stood open on the floor, along with a rag splattered with color. Was he painting again after so long? She glanced around the room looking for the canvas but saw none. At least she wouldn't have to find Beth's face staring back at her from a painting. He'd rarely painted anything else in his last year as an artist before he quit.

She wanted to ask him about his artwork. Often she had prayed that he would be able to get past his old hurts so he could resume painting with the passion and pleasure he once had for it. Unlike many young artists he had a natural talent for capturing light and beauty in his brush strokes, like the Renaissance painters of old. It was almost as though he breathed life into his images, sparking the imagination and emotions of whoever viewed the work.

She was just about to call out and ask him about the paints when she heard a knock at the front door.

"Yoo-hoo! Guy, are you in here?"

Janessa turned and froze, finding Beth Alderman standing in the doorway.

Beth looked as stunning as she had the night of the museum benefit. Her blond hair floated around her shoulders, and her makeup was applied with an expert touch. She hadn't grown fat or ugly with the years as Janessa once wished upon her in a fit of teenage jealousy. No, Beth was as trim and beautiful as ever. Was it a result of natural efforts or the hand of a plastic surgeon? Janessa remembered why Beth and Guy had parted. In comparison Janessa felt sticklike and gauche in her less-than-fashionable clothes.

The two women eyed each other with equal disdain. Beth had never liked Janessa, comparing her to an annoying pest that never stopped buzzing about, and Janessa didn't trust Beth.

She'd hurt Guy once, and she didn't want to see it happen again. Why was Beth at Guy's apartment? Had she been following them, or was she there to model for Guy's painting?

"Nessa, I'm ready now. Thanks for waiting so patiently." Guy stopped short when he saw Beth standing in the doorway. "What are you doing here?" he demanded with a tight frown.

He didn't sound as warm or friendly as Janessa had expected, and it gave her heart a small measure of hope.

"I thought we could talk. It's been a long time since we've been together, and we ought to get reacquainted." Beth's confident smile slipped a fraction when Guy's frown deepened. "But since you're busy giving art lessons or something—"

"Art lessons? If anything, Janessa could teach me a thing or two about painting." He stepped to Janessa's side and wrapped his arm around her waist.

Beth's smile turned into a scowl. She hadn't liked sharing Guy ten years ago, putting Janessa down at every opportunity, and now was no different apparently. Janessa felt as though the three of them had stepped into a scene from the past. Only this time Guy had his arm around a different woman.

"I'm hoping she'll agree to give me art lessons for the rest of my life," he continued as though he were carrying on a casual conversation with a neighbor and not his ex-fiancée.

"What's that supposed to mean? I never did like silly mind games, Guy. Just come out and say whatever it is you're getting at," Beth snapped.

"If Janessa believes it's God's will, she and I are going to get married," he said softly.

"No!" Beth gasped, staring at him in disbelief. When no one said anything to deny Guy's claim her eyes grew stormy. "I know you're just trying to get even with me and make me jealous. How many times do I have to say I'm sorry? Guy, I don't believe for a minute you intend to marry this girl. You and I belong together, and once you stop playing games we can pick up where we left off ten years ago. You have my number. When you come to your senses, give me a call."

"Don't hold your breath," Guy muttered, but Janessa doubted Beth heard his words. She had turned on her heel with a huff and flounced out the door.

"I have my things packed. Are you ready to go?" he asked as though Beth had never been there.

Janessa stared at him in surprise when he didn't comment on Beth's arrival at his apartment or anything she said. She wondered if there was a glimmer of truth to what Beth said. Was Guy using her to make Beth uncomfortable—even jealous—after the way she'd treated him ten years ago? Even though he claimed to want to get married, where was his declaration of love? She couldn't imagine marrying any man except Guy, but without love it wouldn't be a marriage at all. Was it possible he still loved Beth? As long as Beth Alderman stood between them Janessa knew she would never be able to please him.

Back in Guy's car Janessa thought only of the tangled mess. She knew she should pray for a solution. Her heart longed to accept his proposal, wishing her love would be enough for both of them, but her mind argued she needed to be practical. Her parents' marriage was strong because God was in the middle of their relationship and they loved each other deeply. God had always been a part of her friendship with Guy. Could his friendship develop into love?

"We're almost there," Guy murmured, bringing her thoughts to the present. She stared out the window, noticing the familiar neighborhood, and her heart started thumping furiously in her chest.

"Stop the car! I can't let you take me to my grandfather's house."

Guy's grip tightened on the steering wheel, and Janessa could see by the set of his jaw he wasn't going to argue with her. Aside from jumping out of the moving car she had no choice but to comply with his wishes. She threw herself back in the seat and glared out the window.

"I can't stay there, and you know it," she said softly once she got her emotions under control again. There was no use yelling at Guy when her problem was with her grandfather. "I want the Caravaggio to be safe. Can't we find somewhere else?" she asked desperately when he didn't answer.

"I want *you* to be safe, and I can't think of any other place to take you. Don't worry. I'm not going to drop you off and leave you to fend for yourself against Walter. Remember I packed a bag, as well? Think of me as your mediator."

Janessa knew she'd need more than Guy's amateur skills as a go-between to deal with her grandfather. Walter didn't approve of her. She couldn't please him no matter how hard she tried.

It was going to be a long night.

A pounding headache started forming before Janessa even stepped out of the parked car. She knew it was because of stress and dread of facing her grandfather's displeasure. Staying in the car all night was more appealing than being in close quarters with Walter, but she had little choice in the matter, it seemed. Guy thought it best she stay there, and he was probably right. Where else could she go when a stranger was looking for her and the Caravaggio? Even if her grandfather were teamed up with Ted Devroe, he would never hurt her. Her pride would suffer, but she wouldn't be in any danger.

"I'll be there the entire time," Guy promised as he helped

her out of the car. "It'll be just like old times."

Janessa clutched the bag that encased the painting and held it against her like a shield. She felt as if she were going into battle, but her opponent was much stronger and more savvy than she. She'd always been the underdog in skirmishes with her grandfather because he knew how to manipulate her and get the upper hand. She didn't want it to be *just like old times*, but she knew it would. Slowly her feet carried her up the path to the front door.

Before Guy could knock, the door swung open, and her grandfather stood in the doorway, glowering at them.

"I thought you'd come much sooner. It isn't a good idea to gallivant all over town with a priceless painting. Get in here so I can take a look at it." He ushered them inside and locked the door behind them. "You weren't followed?"

Guy shrugged. "I don't think so, but I don't know for certain."

Janessa knew by the scowl on her grandfather's face that he wasn't pleased with Guy's answer, but he didn't say anything. Instead he turned his attention to her.

"You look tired, Janessa. Dark circles under your eyes. I'm sure you've been working too hard."

Janessa wished she could hide her face from his penetrating gaze, but she couldn't so she lifted her chin instead. "You always said hard work was the way to prove myself."

She was surprised when her grandfather rewarded her with something resembling a smile. "I did say that, didn't I? Well, don't just stand there! Bring the painting over here!"

Janessa carefully pulled the Caravaggio from the bag then stripped away the coarse paper Ted had wrapped around it. After propping it on her grandfather's easel she took a step back so he could study it.

Again she was struck by the beauty of the painting, the bold strokes, the play of light across the maiden's face. It made her heart quicken with thankfulness that God had blessed a man so long ago with the talent of translating his world onto canvas. She wondered who the young girl was who had posed so patiently for Michelangelo Merisi da Caravaggio. Had she been his younger sister or perhaps a girl in the local village? Her skin was flawlessly white, her eyes dark and vulnerable, yet a mysterious smile played across her lips. Perhaps Caravaggio loved her as Guy had loved Beth when he painted her portrait. How she longed for him to look on her with that same feeling reflected in his eyes. Did he see the love in her gaze even though she did her best to hide it?

Walter let out a low whistle before switching off the bright lamp that illuminated the canvas. "Now I understand why there's been so much drama."

"What do you mean?"

"The break-in at the museum, someone following you and threatening you—I can see why you would be in danger."

Janessa threw Guy an accusing look but said nothing. She hadn't expected him to confide in her grandfather. It felt almost like a betrayal. "I'm fine. There's nothing to be concerned about," she answered stiffly.

Walter snorted. "Nothing to be concerned about? Don't be dim-witted, girl! Take a look at that painting. It's probably four hundred years old, right? It's worth an incredible amount of money, having never been seen by the public! The only ones who know about it are Ted Devroe, some man leaving threats on your answering machine, and us three. Is that correct?"

Mutely Janessa nodded in answer to his questions.

"Then I'd say we have plenty to be concerned about."

An hour later Guy and Walter locked themselves in the

study, leaving Janessa in the kitchen to entertain herself. They'd had a quick dinner of take-out Chinese. Walter did most of the talking, reminding Janessa and Guy what fabulous artists they had the potential of becoming if they'd just try a little harder. Soon after eating, the men left Janessa alone with the excuse that they had to make plans. She had the suspicion they were making plans for her, and it galled her that she wasn't included in the discussion.

While she fumed she put away the remains of their meal. She would have continued to clean the kitchen, but it was immaculate, thanks to her grandfather's housekeeper.

"Lord, I don't know what they're planning, but I pray that You will be my advocate and guide me. Help me through this evening with my grandfather so I don't say anything I don't mean or take offense at things that aren't important." She wanted to add a prayer that for once she'd be able to please her grandfather, but somehow she felt it would never come true. She didn't want to ask only to be disappointed.

Behind the closed door of the study Janessa heard raised voices, and she knew a moment of fear. If Guy became angry, would he leave her there alone with her grandfather?

Suddenly the study's door swung open, and her grandfather called her into the room. Guy stood by the window looking grim. His lips formed a tight line, and Janessa knew he was angry. She wanted to remind him Walter often said infuriating things that didn't matter. Yet she didn't dare try to comfort him in front of her grandfather who was watching her closely.

"I want you to paint a copy of the Caravaggio," Walter announced.

"What?" Janessa stared at him blankly. He'd hated her ability to copy other works and made her promise never to abuse her talent. They both knew it could lead her into a lot of trouble in the world of art.

"I have everything you need here," he continued as though she understood and agreed with his plan. "I'm sure it will take several days. But we don't have that much time. I suggest you get started immediately."

"Wait a minute! Why do you want me to paint a forgery? I can't do it! I won't paint any more copies, and besides I have my work at the museum to consider—"

"You won't be going back to the museum."

Janessa's stubborn gaze collided with her grandfather's. She didn't want to argue with him, but he had no right to tell her she couldn't go back to her job. It was her job, her life—all of which he didn't approve of anyway. "I have to go back to work. There's so much to be done, and Ted is depending on me to—"

"What do you mean you won't paint any more copies? What other copies have you painted?" her grandfather interrupted.

"I recreated the painting that overlaid this. Ted wanted me to paint a forgery for Mrs. Pembroke so she wouldn't feel as if she lost her painting in the process. He promised to tell her it was a copy."

Her grandfather nodded grimly, his jaw tense. "I see."

"I don't think it's a good idea to copy the Caravaggio," she said stubbornly.

"You've taken—stolen—the original from the museum. You have a curator who makes you paint forgeries, and you have a stranger threatening you. Of course it's a good idea to make a copy. We have to keep the original safe until this situation blows open and the suspects are caught. Otherwise the original painting will slip back into obscurity, and the art thief will still be loose. Be sensible. Your copy will help bring about the end of this."

Janessa realized with horror that what her grandfather accused her of was true. She had stolen the Caravaggio! *Dear Lord, forgive me.* At the time she only considered keeping the painting safe and returning it to its rightful owner. If it remained in the museum, Ted could have done anything with it. She thought the right thing to do was to take it, but was it?

"How will a copy help this situation?" She knew her grandfather was involved, but did he want the original masterpiece for himself? No! Walter was a perfectionist and overly critical, but he wasn't a thief or dishonest.

"We'll return the copy to the museum while I put the original in safekeeping. I suspect it won't take the thief long to recognize he's been duped with a forgery. We'll watch for him to make a mistake—every thief does."

"And in the meantime the situation becomes even more dangerous for Janessa. The thief will be looking for her because he thinks she has the original," Guy interjected. He crossed his arms over his chest, glaring openly at her grandfather. Walter ignored him.

"There's no alternative, so you'd better get busy. We need to get the copy into the museum as soon as possible."

"You don't think Ted will find it suspicious that the painting is missing and I'm not able to come to work?" she asked.

Walter shrugged. "Let me deal with Devroe. I'll tell him I don't approve of my granddaughter working in an unsafe environment since the museum was broken into. And as one of the board members I'll point out a few responsibilities he's been neglecting. That should keep him too busy to worry about you."

Janessa doubted Ted would be so easily distracted, but she knew it was pointless to argue with her grandfather now that he had made up his mind. The easiest course was to comply with him. "If you'll give me the supplies, I'll get started," she said with a sigh of resignation. The sooner she completed this project, the sooner she could get on with her life. Maybe then she and Guy would have a chance to explore their feelings.

# ten

Janessa worked long into the night reproducing the painting. Guy had chosen the bedroom directly across the hall from Walter's studio and could see the light filtering under the door. He felt better knowing she was close by should she need him. But she'd said very little to him since agreeing to do the painting. When he argued it wasn't in Janessa's best interest to be even more involved, she had given him a small, resigned smile. It bothered him that she went along with everything her grandfather had to say. He knew the reason behind it—she was still trying to gain his approval—but it galled him nonetheless. If he were honest with himself, he wanted her to take his side over her grandfather's in this. He wanted to feel they were a team, but instead they were three separate teams perhaps fighting for the same goal.

Long after Walter went to bed, Guy offered to stay up with her while she worked. She merely blinked at him through her glasses, looking like an owl, and told him it wasn't necessary for him to sit with her. She was fine. Guy wanted to argue that she didn't look "fine." Dark shadows circled her eyes. Her shoulders were probably cramped from holding the same position. And by the way she kept rubbing her temples he knew she had a headache. But when he offered any assistance, she merely gave him a tight little smile, if he could call it a smile, and said she was fine. Several times he tried to encourage her to get some sleep, but she ignored him as she bent over the canvas in concentration. Finally he gave up and went to bed, praying for her until he fell asleep.

Around five in the morning he awoke to the sound of someone screaming. Panic thundered in his chest. Someone might be hurting Janessa. He ran toward the bedroom that had belonged to her years ago and was puzzled to find the bed empty. Again a scream sounded from Walter's studio.

Guy found her asleep on the leather sofa. Bright light still glowed from the lamps near the easel, and he guessed she must have sat for just a short break, not intending to fall into such a deep sleep. He approached the sofa on silent feet, but he didn't need to worry. Nothing as soft as footsteps would have awakened her.

Guy stood over Janessa, studying her as she slept. He could see the gray smudges under her eyes where her dark lashes rested, attesting to her exhaustion. Rather than looking peaceful she frowned fiercely, and Guy knew she was having a bad dream. It was no wonder with all the pressure she'd been under. While he debated whether or not to awaken her, she thrashed suddenly on the sofa.

"No, Guy! Look out! He's going to take it! Please don't hurt him!" The last words came out as a sob.

Kneeling beside her, Guy stroked his fingers along her cheek. "Come on, Nessa. Wake up. You're having a nightmare."

She turned her face into his hand, opening her eyes. "Guy?"

"I'm here. Nothing is going to hurt you." And he knew in his heart he would do anything in his power to keep that promise.

"It was awful. I dreamed they were coming for the painting—two faceless people. I couldn't give them what they wanted, so they threatened to hurt you. I couldn't stop them. I was so scared for you."

A single tear traced down her cheek. He felt the moisture

against his fingers where they cupped her face.

"Nothing's going to happen to me. It's you I worry about," he said in a husky whisper.

"I don't know why you care. I'm not trying to sound difficult," she added when he stiffened. "Why me? Why now? I acted like an annoying little sister to you when you were studying under my grandfather. What has changed?"

*Everything and nothing,* Guy wanted to tell her. It was on the tip of his tongue to say that she'd blossomed into a beautiful, talented woman in the years they'd been apart. And yet she was still the same sensitive and kindhearted person. She hadn't changed—he had. In that moment he realized something he'd overlooked while trying to protect her.

He loved her.

He didn't want to marry her because he owed Walter a favor. He needed her and didn't want to spend a single minute away. This was why God had brought them together. She was the one he needed in his life.

"I love. . ." He let the words drop into silence. How could he tell her? Would she even believe him? She was practical and probably wouldn't appreciate sappy poetry from an ex-artist. Instead he said, "You're special, unlike any woman I've ever known. I believe God has brought us together for a second chance, and I won't waste it. I want to spend my life with you."

He saw confusion and uncertainty dart through her eyes. He took her hand in his, hoping to encourage her. Her fingers felt icy cold. Inwardly he prayed she would give him a chance to prove himself to her. "Will you be my wife, Janessa?" he asked softly.

Seconds stretched as she studied his face. A faint blush had risen to her cheeks to chase away the shadows of fatigue. It seemed she would never answer his question.

"What about Beth?"

"Beth is in the past. I want you to be my wife."

Finally she closed her eyes, breathing a gentle sigh, as a small smile played across her lips. "Yes, I'll marry you," she whispered.

Guy pressed a kiss against her forehead. "I love you," he whispered. When she didn't respond he knew she was already asleep.

ᶻᵃ

Janessa slept for a few hours before rousing herself to work on the painting again. When Guy awoke later in the morning and tried to ply her with eggs, toast, and coffee, she adamantly refused. She had to finish the forgery. It wasn't a pleasurable process. Creating something deceptive went against everything in her being, but she knew it was necessary to protect the Caravaggio from theft. If it weren't to help Mrs. Pembroke keep her painting, Janessa would have firmly refused to make the copy. Her grandfather's scheme seemed convoluted. She saw so many uncertainties, but he was convinced it was the only way to prevent the original from being stolen.

"Still working, huh?" Walter grumbled as he stepped into the studio.

Janessa didn't look up or greet him. Anything she said would be taken as a weak excuse, and she was too tired from lack of sleep to do battle with him. Along with the lack of sleep her thoughts were in a whirl, and it was difficult to concentrate on her work. Guy had proposed to her, and she had accepted! She still wasn't sure what he felt in his heart, but she saw something in his gaze that gave her hope. When he first proposed, she'd hesitated only because she wasn't certain of his motives, but last night she found the answer she needed. Effusive words of love and devotion hadn't accompanied his proposal as she would have preferred. Yet duty wasn't the reason for his offer. When she stared into his eyes, she'd been sure he genuinely wanted to marry her. If only he could love her as much as she loved him! She needed to tell him how she felt.

Walter stepped closer and peered over her shoulder at the nearly completed painting. A few places needed extra work, and more finishing touches had to be added. She hoped her grandfather would have the grace to keep silent and allow her to finish without his criticism.

He stood silently, watching her work, but it was impossible to forget he was there. When her hand began to shake she turned with a sigh of frustration. "Did you need me to do something for you?"

Walter looked discomfited by her question. "I'm sorry. I got caught up in watching you. If you'd rather I left the room—"

Janessa stared at him as though he were a stranger. Her grandfather had never apologized to her before. "Uh, no, you don't have to leave. You were making me nervous by standing so close."

"And I was blocking your light, too." Walter strode over to the sofa where Janessa had spent the night and sat down with a sigh. "As soon as you're finished Guy can take it back to the museum. I've already called Devroe and told him you won't be in."

Janessa had to stifle the irritation that rose within her. The Bible said to be slow to anger. "And what did Ted say?" she asked in an indifferent tone that pleased her.

"He was surprised I was the one to call. Otherwise he seemed distracted. I imagine he's discovered the painting is missing and is trying to figure out where you put it."

Janessa thought he was probably right and was glad to be safe in his house. If Ted were responsible for the threats, then he wouldn't dare pursue her when she was under her grandfather's protection.

"When I'm finished I'd like to return the original painting to Mrs. Pembroke. She deserves to have her property," she said as she turned back to the copy. It was nearly finished.

"No."

Janessa turned to stare at her grandfather. "No?"

He didn't look up from the newspaper he'd spread across the coffee table in front of him. "No. The Pembrokes will never touch that painting again."

Janessa felt the fragile peace between them beginning to slip. How dare he call all the shots? She hadn't asked him to step in and take over the situation. Guy wanted her to be safe for the night, so they turned to her grandfather. She didn't like having him in the middle of the conflict, robbing her of all decisions.

Before she could argue with him or demand an explanation, Guy walked into the room carrying two mugs.

"Since you didn't want the coffee, I thought you might like a cup of hot chocolate. It's brisk outside this morning and certainly cold in this studio. No wonder your hands were so cold last night."

Janessa accepted the mug with a murmur of thanks. She knew her grandfather was watching them speculatively and didn't want to explain her relationship with Guy to him. Her grandfather certainly hadn't approved of Guy's choice when he fell in love with Beth, but he hadn't applauded Janessa's teenage crush either. What would he say if Janessa told him she was now engaged to Guy? He would probably scoff at both of them for their foolishness. If she had her way, she wouldn't tell him until the marriage took place.

Unfortunately Guy didn't share her thoughts. "I think you should know, Walter—Janessa has agreed to become my wife." He slipped his arm around her waist as she sat on the stool. She nearly choked on the hot chocolate.

Janessa braced herself for her grandfather's abusive words. When he said nothing, she stared at him in surprise.

"You'll be safe," he finally said, breaking the tense silence. "That's all that matters to me."

This was news to Janessa, and she could say nothing in reply. For the last ten years she hadn't felt very important to her grandfather. Why did he seem concerned now?

Once the painting was finished, she went to her old room and fell into an exhausted sleep. She was too tired to pray or even think about her grandfather's words. She hadn't expected his approval or a nod of satisfaction when she announced the painting was completed. He'd never given effusive praise to anyone so she hadn't anticipated any, but to not receive a word of criticism had been shocking.

❧

Janessa awoke to the sound of voices outside her closed bedroom door. She tried to ignore them and go back to sleep, but it was no use. She peered at the ornate clock on the bedside table. It read three thirty.

Her eyes felt gritty with fatigue. She wasn't accustomed to all the stress and snatches of sleep she'd received. She hoped her grandfather was right and the copy would bring about the end of the turmoil in her life.

As she searched for a clean T-shirt and jeans in her overnight bag she could hear her grandfather's raised voice. Whenever anyone disagreed with him he raised his voice. Normally she wouldn't think much of it, but under the circumstances it was important for her to know everything that was being discussed. Most likely she was the center of the conversation.

Abandoning the idea of a long hot shower, Janessa slipped into her clothes, pulled her hair back in a simple ponytail and shoved her feet in sneakers similar to what she wore as a teenager. Refusing to glance in the mirror, she hurried from her room to learn what her grandfather was planning. By the time she reached the kitchen Walter was alone.

"So Sleeping Beauty finally decided to drag herself out of bed," he muttered by way of a greeting when she found him in the kitchen.

Janessa ignored his surly comment, wishing for the glimmer of approval she'd witnessed earlier in the day. She went over to the refrigerator and grabbed a soda. "What's the next step in this devious plan of yours?"

"This isn't a game, Janessa! Your life could have been in danger without my help, and I wish you would take this more seriously."

He was right, Janessa knew, but she didn't want him making all the decisions. Yet arguing with him was pointless when his mind was set. He wanted to finalize the arrangements and leave her on the sidelines. "Where's Guy?"

"He's taking care of something for me. He'll be right back, and you can go with him to take the forgery to the museum. I'm sure it would be pointless to insist you stay here."

Janessa only halfway listened to her grandfather as a nagging suspicion began to form in the back of her mind. Something was going on that he wasn't telling her about. Without explanation she left her grandfather alone in the kitchen and went to his study where she had worked on the painting. Upon the easel sat the forgery as she'd left it, but the original was gone.

She didn't waste any time looking for it. She hurried back to the kitchen where Walter sipped a cup of coffee. He didn't even look up when she stood in the doorway glaring at him.

"You've taken it, haven't you?"

Still he didn't look up. "Yes."

"Where? Where is the original Caravaggio? You knew I wanted to return it to Mrs. Pembroke. How could you take it while I was sleeping? Of course I couldn't argue when I didn't have a clue what you were up to. Is that where Guy is now? Taking care of the painting for you?"

The more she railed at her grandfather, the more suspicions formed in her mind. Was he involved in selling it? He might have been working with Ted all along. When Ted refused to cooperate, Walter took matters into his own hands and used Janessa's talent for forgery to pass off a fake on Ted. Did that mean Guy was involved, as well? He didn't reappear in her life until just before the Caravaggio was discovered. And he'd been hired by Ted at the museum upon her grandfather's insistence. A sick feeling began to roil in the pit of Janessa's stomach as she stared at her grandfather in horror. Had she been played a fool by all of them?

It felt like a knotted web of deceit that kept growing more complicated at every turn. The more she tried to unravel it, the more condemning information she received. Could she trust anyone?

What was she thinking? Of course she could trust Guy! He'd never given her any reason to doubt him. Even though everything was confusing she knew Guy wasn't involved in stealing the painting. Yet did she have the same confidence in her grandfather?

"Wipe that look off your face, Janessa," Walter ordered. "I didn't take the painting for my own purposes, and shame on you for suspecting me."

Janessa didn't know how he knew her thoughts except that she'd never been able to hide a secret from him, even as a child. A warm flush of guilt crept up her neck and into her cheeks, and it was difficult to return his gaze. "I heard you on the phone with Ted. He talked to you about getting rid of the painting. After hearing that, of course I suspected you. I'm very confused right now. It seems everyone I know is involved with this somehow."

"And that's why I'm trying to protect you."

"How do I know you're not on the wrong side of this? Would you take it? I need to know the truth."

Walter gazed at her. "I promise you with a solemn oath that I would never steal and resell someone's painting. It's in a safe place to protect you, its owner, and everyone involved until this is finished."

She returned his gaze, wanting to believe him.

Footsteps echoed in the hall, and her grandfather brightened at the sound. "Ah, good, here's Guy. Now he can return to the museum with the copy."

Janessa turned to see Guy standing behind her. Her heart did a flip at the sight of him. Their gazes met, and she felt an overwhelming flood of love. Could he see how she reacted to him? If they were alone she would tell him how she felt; but her grandfather was standing nearby, and they had to deal with the forgery. "How will you get the new painting into my workroom? Only Ted, Rosy, and I have keys. You need me to go with you." She knew it could be dangerous.

Guy's gaze moved beyond her, and she had the feeling he was seeking her grandfather's advice on the matter. She wanted to tell both of them that she didn't need their permission, but she would have been lying. Guy was going to be her husband.

She wanted his approval as desperately as she wanted her grandfather's—no matter how tough she pretended to be.

Finally Guy sighed. "All right, Janessa, you can come with me. But I don't like the idea one bit."

# eleven

"Stay close to me," Guy murmured as they moved down the rear hallway of the museum. The building was still open to the public, but no one was allowed in the administrative side without permission. Ted didn't know they were there, but he'd only have to look at the security monitors to learn of their movements.

"Don't fidget. Try to look normal," Guy whispered as he glanced toward one of the security cameras. He clutched Janessa's fingers tightly in his. They felt like ice, just like the night before when he'd proposed. Were her hands always this cold, or was she just nervous? By the sound of her shallow breathing he knew she was scared, and he wished again she hadn't come. She didn't need to be there. He could have snuck the painting in himself and gotten out without detection. She should have given him the key, but he understood her stubbornness. It wasn't a question of trust on her part; she simply wanted to see this to the end.

*Let that end come soon, Lord,* he prayed. He wanted to resume a normal life—one that would include Janessa by his side every day, knowing she was safe.

"Do you have the keys?" she whispered. She had given him the keys on the drive over to the museum and had asked him twice since they entered the building.

"I have the keys, and it's going to be fine." They reached her workroom, and Guy shifted the painting into Janessa's hands so he could unlock the door. Once inside with the door closed firmly behind them she gave an audible sigh of relief. She switched on the small lamp on her desk. It was just enough to illuminate the room in shadowy light.

"I'll put the painting where I found it, and then we can get out of here."

Guy watched her cross the room to the canvases stacked against the wall. As he waited he felt a prickling sensation along the back of his neck. Everything seemed to be moving in slow motion, and they were taking too long. Behind him he sensed rather than heard the door open.

"Stop what you're doing!" Ted ordered.

Janessa gasped, and Guy was afraid she'd drop the painting; but she clutched it tightly like a shield in front of her.

"Put the painting back where you found it. I won't let you take it."

"You can't hide the Caravaggio in here, Ted. Its value may be beyond calculation, but that doesn't give you the right to keep the painting from its rightful owner. Let me take it to Mrs. Pembroke."

"And were you going to walk out of here with a valuable masterpiece and take it to a little woman with blue hair and an attic full of ugly artwork? Do you really trust her? She's the last person who should have this painting. I won't let you do it." Ted strode into the room. He walked over to Janessa and tried to take the painting from her hands, but she held it away. Guy sucked in his breath, praying Ted wouldn't detect it was a forgery.

"What are you going to do with it?" Janessa demanded.

Ted seemed frustrated that she refused to hand over the painting. "I'm not going to sell it. I'm just trying to do the right thing—like you, Janessa." When she didn't move or respond he scowled at her. "Don't you think your actions look just as suspicious? I should call the cops or throw you out of here for good. You never would have acted like this before he showed up." Ted gestured toward Guy as though he were trash in the gutter. "Didn't I tell you to stay away from him?"

"I'm going to marry him, Ted," she answered softly.

Ted's scowl deepened with this news. "You're making a big mistake, Janessa. Be practical! How do you know he's everything he appears?"

Janessa's gaze met Guy's. She wasn't questioning him so he didn't have to defend himself. Yet he could say nothing anyway. He couldn't convince her Ted was wrong. He *wasn't* everything he appeared. Her grandfather had hired him to protect her. He was there under false pretenses, assuming the role of custodian and long-lost friend. If Walter hadn't called him, he wouldn't be back in Janessa's life. Yet none of those things mattered because he loved her. It may have begun for the wrong reasons, but what he felt and believed now was right.

He wanted to tell her everything, but he couldn't break his promise to Walter and tell her why he was there—not yet anyway. And with Ted standing between them it wasn't the moment for confession.

"What about us, Janessa?" Ted persisted. "If you're trying to make me jealous, it's working. I planned for you to marry me—remember? Or did you think I was joking? I thought you'd make the perfect deacon's wife, though looking at you now in those ratty jeans and T-shirt I don't know why I ever thought that."

Guy couldn't listen to another minute of Ted's abuse. "You, like the Pharisees, can only focus on the outside of the cup. Jesus said to clean the inside. Janessa has more inner—and outer—beauty than anyone I know. Who cares about clothes?

If you can't see the truth, then you certainly don't deserve her. *I* don't deserve her." He strode over to Janessa, took the forgery of the Caravaggio from her hands and propped it on an easel. "Do what you will with the painting. But leave my future wife out of it."

❧

Janessa followed Guy out of the museum, hurrying to keep pace with him. She knew he was angry with Ted. Was everything he said true? She always wanted him to think she was beautiful, but she was more inclined to agree with Ted's assessment of her appearance. She didn't look spectacular—certainly not as noteworthy as Beth Alderman—but Guy seemed to approve of her.

Funny how her first concern was over Guy's opinion of her and not the fact that they'd both probably lost their jobs. Ted expected excellence from everyone in his employ. What he'd just received was a blow to his ego. It wasn't Janessa's fault he had difficulty separating the personal from the professional in his life. And when it came to professionalism she had a few sins of her own. Not once did she admit Ted was wrong in assuming they were trying to take the masterpiece. Ted had no idea he now possessed a painstakingly created forgery.

"Janessa! Janessa, stop!" Ted called just as she and Guy reached his car. Janessa could see by the scowl on Guy's face that he would prefer to hop in the car and speed away before Ted reached them. But they both stood immobile as he approached them.

Janessa held her breath and waited for him to expose her as a fraud, but he didn't. "Come back to my office so we can talk. You can't just drop a bombshell and then take off. Come back. I want to say some things, but I don't want to share them in the parking lot."

"No." Guy stepped closer to Janessa and encircled her shoulders with his arm.

Ted's lip curled at Guy's protectiveness. "I'd like to speak to Janessa alone—with your permission, of course," he added.

For the first time in their acquaintance Ted didn't seem so pompous. Was he telling the truth, or was it a ruse to get information from her about the painting? With any luck he might accidentally give her some useful information instead. "I could talk to him for just a minute." Her gaze met Guy's as she silently pleaded with him to agree. If he stayed close she would be safe enough. Finally he nodded.

"I don't like this," he murmured as they followed Ted back into the building. "What if this is a trick?"

"You'll be right here with me, and nothing can go wrong," she whispered. She took his hand in hers and held tightly. "I know I'll be safe."

They reached Ted's office, and he ushered her inside. Guy stood on the threshold, and she knew he wanted to follow her.

"I'll be waiting right outside for you, Janessa. I'm here if you need me." His words comforted her, but she knew they were given as a warning to Ted.

"Nothing's going to happen, Langly," Ted retorted as he shut the door in Guy's face. "Except I'm going to talk her out of this nonsense," he added.

Janessa sat stiffly across from the desk. Rather than circling to sit in his big leather chair like a king upon his throne, Ted pulled up another chair and sat knee to knee with her. She inched back uncomfortably, trying to add millimeters of space between them.

"I get the idea you're trying to punish me," he muttered with a glance toward the door.

Janessa sat primly with her hands clasped in her lap. "I don't know why you're saying that."

"You knew I didn't like Langly, and now you're going to marry him. All the trouble with the Caravaggio and the museum break-in began when he took the job here. I think you're doing this just to get my attention. If you end this charade, I'll forgive you."

"Charade? My engagement doesn't have anything to do with you. And what do you mean the trouble started when he took the job? Are you accusing Guy of trying to steal the painting?"

"No! No." Ted took hold of Janessa's hand. "I'm not accusing anyone, even though I caught you with the painting in your hands. But we're not talking about the painting. I think you've made a hasty and impractical decision. I've told you before you would make the perfect wife of a deacon. I had planned to take things slower and help you along. Then Langly showed up and ruined everything between us. Can't you see you're not well suited? What do you have in common with him?"

Janessa knew it was pointless to explain her relationship with Guy. Ted didn't want to understand because it interfered with his plans. But they didn't share the same desires. She wanted Guy to be her husband. It was all she'd ever hoped and prayed for; she refused to be moved by Ted's attempt to shake her faith. God had brought Guy back into her life for a reason, and she wouldn't let him go. It didn't matter what things Ted rattled off in his assault against Guy. She knew him and was confident he had nothing to do with the Caravaggio. But she didn't have the same faith in Ted.

"I'm sorry you believed there could be something between us. We work together, that's all. Perhaps you misunderstood, or maybe I wasn't clear. I've only wanted to be friends."

"You say 'friends,' but what woman doesn't want designer clothes, a nice car, a fancy house? I can give you all those things. You can't marry him." Before Janessa could protest Ted pulled her toward him and forced a kiss on her lips. When she struggled to be free he immediately released her.

Janessa was about to protest his rough actions, but someone behind them—a woman—cleared her throat.

"Ah, excuse me. I knocked, but since the door was slightly open. . .I didn't mean to interrupt—"

Janessa turned in horror to stare at Beth Alderman who returned Janessa's gaze with a satisfied smirk. But it was Guy's fierce scowl that caught and held her attention.

❧

As Guy stood in the hallway, he could hear Janessa and Ted—though he couldn't make out their conversation. He was concerned with her safety. But, more important, was Ted trying to persuade her to end the engagement? As the museum curator, Ted could be smooth and persuasive. Guy knew she didn't want a relationship with the man, but would she listen to him? He was still trying to decide whether or not to interrupt the conversation when Beth walked into the museum.

His heart sank when he caught sight of her. He wanted to avoid all contact with her, but he stood his ground near the office door. When she paused in the doorway to reapply her lipstick, he knew she had spotted him. She fluffed her blond hair around her shoulders so it floated like a golden cloud. Even though he couldn't see her eyes behind the dark sunglasses, he knew her gaze was fixed on him. He felt like the "catch of the day," and Beth was the fisher who intended to reel him in. Did it matter to her that he was no longer interested? Rather than wait for her to approach Guy moved away from the door and met her halfway.

"Oh, hello. I didn't see you standing there," Beth murmured in her sultry voice.

*Now try telling the truth for once, Beth,* he thought but kept the words unspoken. Starting a verbal sparring match with her would serve no purpose.

She trailed her long red fingernails down his sleeve. "I don't believe it's a coincidence—meeting here at the museum, twice like this. I think it's a sign. We belong together. Think what a boost it would be! My agent can market us: 'Beth and Guy Together Again—Better than Before,' or 'The Past Revisited.'"

Guy shook his head in disbelief. "You've obviously given this a lot of consideration. I don't see why you need me to help revive your career."

"I told you this before, Guy," Beth said. "We go together like Romeo and Juliet, chocolate and peanut butter, shopping and credit cards. We were *meant* to be together."

Guy didn't appreciate her analogies, and he certainly didn't agree with them. "I'm sorry, Beth, but your plan to use me in reviving your modeling career won't happen. You'll have to rely on your looks."

Beth's gaze narrowed dangerously, and Guy knew her temper was flaring. She'd slapped him once, leaving long marks across his cheek from her manicured nails. How had he cared for her so blindly? She'd fooled him by going to his church and pretending to be the wonderful person he thought she was. Just because she grew up in a Christian home didn't mean she held to his same values. Success had meant more to her then, and obviously now, than anything Guy said or believed in.

"Are you refusing me because of that twit you're hanging around with again? She's going nowhere, Guy, and the sooner you realize it the better off you'll be. I know you were just teasing me when you said you're going to marry her. Your plan worked. I was furious all day. But it also made me realize how much I want you—how much I *need* you. So forget this nonsense. Stop being angry and come back to me, Guy. Besides, I have a little secret. I actually stopped here to donate one of the pieces you did. It's to be a 'reintroduction.' Aren't you happy?"

Guy ground his teeth in frustration, wishing he'd never seen Beth Alderman, now or ten years earlier. She'd done nothing but wreak havoc in his life from the day they met. He didn't know how he could convince her they didn't have a future together. Whenever she set her heart on something she hung on stubbornly until she won. But this time she wouldn't be the victor because Guy had no intention of allowing her chaos back into his life. He wanted to rest in the peace God had for him, and Beth played no part in that plan. He loved Janessa, and she was the only one he wanted to share his life with. The thought of growing old with her gave him a lot of satisfaction.

"Beth, you may have shared the spotlight briefly because of my art, since your face covered every canvas I painted back then. But today is a different day. I'm a different person now, and so are you. Forget the painting you want to donate and toss aside your silly plans. You don't need me anymore. You haven't thought of me in the last ten years. We want different things. You have to chase your own dreams, and I'm going after mine. Separately. I don't love you. I'm in love with Janessa, and I won't have you talking about her like this anymore."

Beth pressed her lips in a narrow line as she glared at Guy. Looking at her, he wondered how he ever found her appealing.

"Just tell me this. Are you painting again?"

The question caught Guy off guard. He didn't want to discuss his artwork with her. She didn't have any privilege knowing what he was doing with his life, and it felt as if she was prying. Whenever she drew information out of people she used it for her own purposes. He didn't know the reason she asked him, and he was leery of answering her. Only Janessa had the right to know his hopes and dreams and whether or not he was painting again.

"By the guilty look on your face I know the truth. You want the spotlight for yourself, and you don't want me to be a part of it because I'm too old. Admit it. I was beautiful ten years ago, but now you don't want to paint me because I've aged. Fine! I'll find my own way. I'll show you I can be a success!"

Before he knew her intentions, Beth stomped toward Ted's office and threw the door open. He caught up just in time to see Ted kissing Janessa.

☙

"It's not how it looks!" Janessa tried to explain, but by the stony expression on Guy's face she doubted he heard her. To make matters worse Beth let out an irritating little giggle. She could only imagine what twisted conclusions everyone was arriving at and knew there was no point in trying to defend herself—not when she wouldn't be heard.

What was Beth doing at the museum anyway? And how could Janessa make Guy understand Ted's kiss had been an insult and nothing more? She stood and forced her voice to be calmer than she felt. "I need to stop by my workroom for a minute." It was only an excuse to get out of the office, but no one else knew that. She brushed past Beth without looking again at the woman's smug expression and paused beside Guy. "Please come with me?"

"I'm coming, too. You're the reason I'm here," Beth announced, and Janessa swallowed a groan.

"I thought you said you were donating a painting," Guy ground out. "Besides, haven't you said enough already?"

"Oh, I'm just getting started!" she retorted. "This museum is like a soap opera," she continued as they walked to Janessa's workroom. The lack of response didn't deter her. "Imagine, a love triangle with an old flame, a museum curator, and a silly little girl."

Guy's fists balled at his sides, but Janessa put her hand on his arm to restrain him from answering. Beth was trying to get a reaction, but she wouldn't get it if Janessa could help it.

"What do you want, Beth?"

"I want to talk to you. It's just a little girl talk, and we don't need Guy in here with us." She turned and gave him one of her pleading, pouting looks that had once been plastered across magazine covers. With her full lips, large blue eyes, and curvaceous figure she had every man wrapped around her finger during the prime of her career. "Wait outside for us?"

When Guy crossed his arms over his chest and stubbornly stood his ground, Janessa was relieved. "I'll stay right here. Anything you have to say to her, you can say to me, as well," he stated firmly.

Janessa crossed to her desk and began arranging papers. She could feel Beth's gaze boring into her back. She prayed that God would give her the right words to say as she reminded herself she didn't have to please Beth. She hadn't been able to gain Beth's friendship years ago, and there was no point in belittling herself now.

"Fine, have it your way. This is where you work?" Beth asked, addressing Janessa. With her nose wrinkled in distaste she walked slowly around the room. She paused to look at the paintings in various stages of restoration.

Janessa didn't bother to answer as she watched Beth. She tried not to compare herself to the glamorous woman, but it was difficult. She was thankful Guy was there with her. He wouldn't leave her.

"I've taken an interest in art myself," Beth continued. She wandered toward the stack of canvases. Janessa stiffened as Beth slowly picked out the Caravaggio forgery from the stack and drew it away from the others. She pulled back the paper and set it on an easel.

"Put that back!"

Beth ignored Janessa's command. "I thought if I became more interested in art, Guy would want me back." She glanced in his direction and then away. "I've done a lot of studying on the subject. I can't tell you who the artist was that painted this, but I can tell you it looks to be from either the late Renaissance to early baroque period. Am I right?"

"It's baroque," Janessa whispered, every sense on alert. Why was she curious? Was it a coincidence she had chosen the Caravaggio out of the stack?

"This is a very expensive piece, isn't it?"

"What do you want, Beth?"

Beth whirled to face Janessa, her eyes flashing. "Guy doesn't love you—how could he? Why would he want to marry you?" She talked as though he wasn't in the room with them. "You have nothing in common, so I'm sure he's doing it out of pity. He always felt sorry for you. I remember him calling you an ugly duckling, and he was right."

"I never said that!" Guy protested, but Beth cut him off with a sharp look.

"You wanted to marry me, remember? How can you be interested in her after knowing me?"

Janessa stood against the desk, trembling with anger as she strained to hear Guy's answer. Beth had asked the same question that had played through her own thoughts over and over.

"I was a fool ever to have feelings for you. Loving Janessa has shown me the truth. There's nothing you can say or do to make me change my mind. And I won't allow you to stand here and insult my fiancée. You need to leave, Beth, and never come back."

Beth brushed her hair from her shoulder with a haughty sweep of her hand, looking every inch the supermodel she once was as she turned back to Janessa. "You'll never be able to please him."

"You're wrong!" Guy said.

"You're just mad at me, aren't you?" she asked as she took a step toward him. She gave him a sad smile with her pouting red lips. "This is all a silly misunderstanding, and we'll get back together. Tell her you don't want to marry her, and you'll be released from your sense of obligation."

"The only obligation I have is to make Janessa understand how I feel about her."

"Which is only pity," Beth added firmly. "You're wasting your time on her since she has feelings for her boss. Remember the lush little kiss we witnessed?" She moved toward the door with her practiced walk. She turned suddenly and gazed at Janessa. "You know he's painting again, don't you?" she asked. Her expression was innocent, but the words were daggers. "I'll be going now."

Janessa sank into the chair beside her desk—the desk Guy had repaired for her. She knew he was painting again, but to hear it from Beth was more hurtful than words could describe. Why hadn't he told her himself? He hadn't touched a paintbrush to canvas since the day Beth broke his heart. If he was painting again, that meant he was finally ready to move on with his life. And the fact that Beth knew about it spoke volumes to her.

"How does she know you're painting again?"

# twelve

Guy could tell by the stricken look on Janessa's face that she felt as miserable as he did. He couldn't get the image of Ted kissing her out of his thoughts. Had Ted surprised her with the kiss, or had she invited it? He couldn't believe she was attracted to another man when she had agreed to marry him, but he had seen the kiss with his own eyes.

"Do you have feelings for Ted Devroe?"

"No! He tried to convince me not to marry you, and when I wouldn't listen he kissed me. That's when Beth burst into the room."

"I've never been so upset as when I saw him holding you."

"But I didn't want him to! He just did it, and I wasn't able to stop him right away because I was so surprised. You believe me, don't you? There's never been anything between Ted and me, and there never will be."

"I believe you," he murmured as he traced his finger down her cheek. He needed to believe her.

She stared at him intently, with sadness in her eyes. "You're painting again, and Beth knows." She sounded so forlorn that Guy wanted to take her in his arms and hold her until she felt better. But he knew it would take more than a hug to comfort her and convince her of the truth.

"Yes." By her crestfallen look Guy knew it wasn't the answer she hoped to hear. He was angry Beth had used the information to hurt her. He wanted her to be happy. Of all the people he knew, Janessa had been the most disappointed

144

when he quit painting.

"How does she know? She isn't your model again, is she?" She stared at him like a wounded child betrayed by someone she trusted.

"Let me show you. Just as Ted wronged you, Beth has wronged me. They both want to undermine our relationship, but I won't let them. Please trust me."

He drove directly to his apartment, and Janessa was silent the entire time. He knew she was wrestling with what Beth had said. He led her into the apartment and told her to wait by his easel while he went to his room to retrieve the canvas. He returned to the living room, his heart thudding nervously. He hadn't wanted to show her the painting yet. It wasn't finished, and he wasn't sure how she would respond. But he couldn't live with the misunderstanding between them.

He placed the canvas on the easel where the bright light from the windows gave the colors a perfect glow. He was proud of his work yet critical, too. He never felt he could accurately portray a person's thoughts or mood on canvas. So many dynamics were impossible to convey.

"Please look, Nessa," he said when she kept her gaze averted. She stood looking out the window as the light created a halo around her. He wished now he could paint her as she stood. He would never compare himself with Michelangelo Merisi da Caravaggio, but Janessa would far outshine the young maiden in the painting.

Slowly Janessa turned. She seemed reluctant to look at the canvas yet compelled to do so. Was she afraid to see Beth's face staring back at her? With a gasp she stepped nearer, her eyes round with wonder.

"It's me," she whispered.

When Guy pulled her into his arms, she didn't resist.

"There's no one—not Beth or any other woman—I want to paint or spend the rest of my life with except you. Only you, Janessa. Will you believe me when I tell you how much I love you? You're in my thoughts and in my heart. I want to be with you always."

"I'll never be as beautiful or glamorous as Beth. How could I ever make you happy?"

"Stop comparing yourself to Beth. I've never done that, and if I did, she would be the one found lacking. You *are* beautiful."

"But I don't dress like everyone else. Makeup, contacts, fashion—I've never had a flair for any of it."

"You can change all those things if they bother you, but they aren't important to me. It's not the frame that makes a painting beautiful. I don't care if you wear a clown suit or an evening gown. I love the person you are and wouldn't change a thing."

"Really?"

"Really. You don't have to do anything to please me because I'm already happy with who you are. Now let's go get our marriage license before you start doubting me again."

But neither of them moved away as they shared a gentle, heartfelt kiss.

❧

Janessa couldn't have been happier that night as she prepared for bed. They were back at her grandfather's house because Guy didn't think it was safe for her to be alone at her apartment, and she agreed. When they had left Guy's apartment to go get their marriage license, they had found a note stuffed under the windshield wiper blade of his car.

*I know you have the painting, and I grow tired of waiting. While I find forgeries amusing, I'm rapidly losing patience. Return the original or suffer the consequences.*

The note had put a damper on their festive mood, reminding Janessa that she still wasn't safe. Guy didn't want her to read it—she knew he was protecting her—but she insisted on seeing it. The pinched bold letters seemed familiar. It wasn't like Ted's, but he could have tried to disguise his handwriting.

One thing was certain: Her carefully painted forgery had been discovered, and the art thief wasn't happy about it.

After receiving this last threat Guy insisted they take the note to the police. This time they didn't have a lengthy question-and-answer session. The officer assured Janessa they were working on the case and encouraged her to be cautious. They could do little else. Janessa didn't need the warning. Ever since the first threat in the parking lot, her life had become one of caution. Guy made sure of that. She knew if he wasn't continually with her the thief probably would have contacted her in person much sooner. Would he have hurt her to get the painting?

Janessa forced all thoughts of the Caravaggio away and tried to focus on Guy and their upcoming wedding ceremony. It was to be simple, at his sister's small church across town. She knew the pastor from a convention she had attended. She only wished her parents could be there.

When she called their answering service, she found they were no longer in the Mediterranean but were now in Japan. She dialed the number to their Japanese hotel and waited for the operator to put the call through to their room.

Her mother answered on the second ring.

"Mom! Why are you in Japan? I thought you were coming home in a few weeks."

"Oh, darling, I'm so glad you caught me! We thought we could squeeze in a special assignment before returning to

New York as scheduled, but this afternoon your father had a nasty fall. Right now they're putting pins in his leg to hold everything together. But he'll be fine—don't you worry. I was going to call you as soon as the doctors finished."

Janessa listened in horror. Her mother had a knack for making everything sound light and uncomplicated, but she knew her father must be in great pain. "Should I fly over?"

"No, no! He'll be fine. If anything, he feels foolish for tumbling down the stairs like a rubber ball. You stay there, and I hope it won't be too long until we get back."

"Mom, I wanted you to know that Guy and I are getting married. I want you to be here. We could put it off a few weeks, but neither of us wants to wait—" She didn't add that they both felt anxious about her safety. Her parents would only worry. "I'm sure I sound perfectly ridiculous—"

"Oh, Janessa! I'm so happy for you! And, no, you're not ridiculous for being in a hurry to marry. I would worry if you felt reluctant. I want to be there very much. But you can't put your life on hold. Marry Guy with our blessing, darling. We've always loved him and known he was special. I'll tell your father as soon as he's finished with the doctors."

"It won't be a fancy ceremony. Simple—"

"Simple and beautiful. If God is in the middle, a small ceremony is as important and honorable as a wedding that costs thousands of dollars. I just want you to be happy. I wish we could be there, but we'll be with you in your heart. You know that. It would be selfish of me to expect you to hold off your wedding day. You've postponed enough things in your life because of our travels. So marry the man you love, and when we return, we'll celebrate with you."

After talking with her mom Janessa felt confident about marrying Guy. Her parents understood and approved of her decision; they'd always trusted her to follow her heart and do the right thing. Even though her grandfather was surly and grumbled through the evening, nothing could dampen Janessa's mood. For once she didn't even try to appease him. Tomorrow she and Guy were getting married, just as she'd always hoped and prayed, and he loved her. It didn't matter what Beth said or how Ted felt. Janessa knew Guy was the husband God had chosen for her, and she loved him.

ⵣⴰ

Janessa sat next to Guy in the backseat while her grandfather drove them to the church. She shifted nervously, smoothing the wrinkles from her cream-colored skirt. It wasn't warm enough for a pretty white sundress, and she hadn't felt an elaborate gown of satin and lace was the right thing for her. So she chose something simple to be married in—a straight skirt that whispered around her ankles and a blouse so silky soft that she felt feminine and pampered wearing it. She wore her hair curled and piled on her head much the same way she had for the museum benefit. Tiny silk flowers were tucked into her hair and matched the simple spray pinned to her blouse. She wore a little makeup, chose contacts in favor of her glasses and decided she had done pretty well on her own—but she wished her mom or even Rosy was there to help her.

Even though her parents couldn't be there, Rosy promised to meet them at the church.

As she shifted again her shoulder bumped Guy.

"Relax—you look beautiful," he whispered in her ear as he caught hold of her hand. Janessa turned to look at him, and the glimmer in his eyes was enough to make her heart trip over itself. No man had ever looked at her with such admiration. She hoped she'd be able to make him happy. Part of her still wondered if this was really happening. It seemed too fanciful, too surreal, to be marrying the man she'd always dreamed of. If she pinched herself, would she wake up to find it was a dream?

Her grandfather pulled up to the church. Guy helped her out of the car and tucked her arm through his so they could walk inside together. At the entrance Guy's parents, his sister, Sara, her husband, Alex, and the girls were waiting. Rosy was there, too, standing beside a man Janessa had never seen. She almost didn't recognize her friend at first. Her hair was cut short above her shoulders, and it was a soft brown almost the same color as Janessa's.

Anna and Jaena immediately demanded the attention of their adoring uncle. While Guy bent to talk with his two nieces, Janessa joined Rosy.

"You look good, Rosy!" she exclaimed, giving her friend a hug.

"You think so? It's my natural color. I haven't seen it for years." Not only was her hair different, but she also wore less makeup and her clothes were demure. Janessa wondered if the stranger next to Rosy was responsible for the changes. "But enough about me! I can't believe you're getting married! I knew Guy Langly was someone special to you, but I had no idea things would move so quickly."

Janessa hadn't told Rosy about the painting or her relationship with Guy. So much had happened in the time she had been in Syracuse with her aunt. How could she sum up everything without causing Rosy undue concern?

"I've known him for years so it doesn't feel that quick to me. But I'm sure it seems completely out of character to everyone who knows me. My parents are happy and my grandfather, too, but Ted wasn't too thrilled about it."

"I'm not surprised. He actually called me at my aunt's house to ask what I thought of it. I told him that if God approved how could I disapprove? That certainly quieted him," Rosy said with an impish grin.

Janessa didn't want to dwell on the fact that Ted was going behind her back to undermine her relationship with Guy. "And how is your aunt?"

The smile slowly faded from Rosy's lips. "Not so well, but she's getting stronger every day. She really needs me there. Greg thinks she's doing better—oh, Janessa, this is Greg! He's my aunt's next-door neighbor. And, well, he's a special friend."

By the unprecedented blush that filled Rosy's cheeks, Janessa guessed her friend was head over heels in love with Greg. Before she could ask more Guy stepped up to her side and put his arm around her waist.

"Sorry to interrupt, but the pastor is urging us to begin the ceremony."

Since it was such a small wedding, Janessa didn't have a maid of honor and Guy didn't have a best man. They had their closest friends and family there to share the occasion, and that was enough to please them. Because her father was injured and lying in a hospital bed in Japan, her grandfather had offered to walk her down the aisle and give her away.

As they waited to step into the sanctuary, her grandfather grasped her hand tightly in his. "I know we've had our differences and have disagreed on most things, but I highly approve of your decision to marry Guy. He's a good man. He'll keep you safe."

Janessa sighed softly, wishing she could change her grandfather's viewpoint. She was glad he approved, but she wanted him to see that Guy was more than a bodyguard to her. He was the one God had chosen for her lifelong mate, and they loved each other.

Before she could respond he led her toward the doorway and up the aisle to where Guy and the pastor waited. Janessa's gaze locked with Guy's, and she searched for any uncertainty or dread and was relieved to find none. He seemed to watch her just as carefully. She hoped he was comforted by everything he found in her gaze as she stared at him with all the love she held in her heart.

The aisle seemed to stretch forever, but finally she reached Guy's side. As her grandfather stepped away and Guy took her hand in his, nothing else seemed to matter. Here was the man God had chosen for her. And today it was being made right between them.

The ceremony passed quickly, and after Janessa uttered her vows to love Guy forever, he slipped a narrow gold band embedded with diamonds on her finger. She'd never seen the ring before, but it was perfect—simple yet elegant as she preferred. It was a symbol that Guy really did know her.

Once the pastor announced them as husband and wife their friends and family gathered around. Guy's parents hugged her effusively. She'd met them before, and they confirmed how happy they were that Guy had chosen her. While the twins were taking turns hugging Janessa, she noticed her grandfather had pulled Guy aside and they were moving toward the rear exit of the sanctuary.

She knew her grandfather had a tendency to put people in a corner. She didn't want him to pressure Guy, whether about his artwork or his choice in careers, so she decided to follow and planned to intervene if necessary. Of course Guy could handle her grandfather, but she didn't want him to agree to anything he didn't want.

They'd stepped outside, and when Janessa pushed the door open slightly she could hear their voices.

"You've made it right, and I owe you for that. I know you'll keep her safe as we agreed," her grandfather said.

Perplexed, Janessa stood woodenly, unable to move forward or pull away. It didn't enter her mind that it was a conversation not meant for her ears.

"I know what I agreed to in the beginning, but the arrangement has changed."

"What? You want more money now? You want me to pay you for marrying my granddaughter as I told you to?" Walter blustered, his voice growing louder. "I hired you to take care of her. I know you weren't keen on the idea at first, but I expect you to stick to our agreement whether you married her or not—"

Janessa couldn't listen to any more. She stepped back into the church, letting the door slip silently back in place. Her stomach lurched violently, and she thought she might be sick. Her grandfather's words were stuck in her mind, playing over and over at a rapid pace as she backed away from the door.

*I hired you to take care of her. . .I know you weren't keen at first. . .I hired you. . .I hired you. . . .*

Guy and Walter had deceived her.

Guy didn't love her. He was hired to protect her—a job he didn't want. Her grandfather was using Guy to interfere in her life. They weren't pleased with her or her choices. To them she was a wayward child needing guidance. How did it go so far? Her grandfather had told Guy to marry her and he agreed? How could she have been so stupid? She thought Guy loved her, and all the time he was doing a job for her grandfather.

As the depth of their betrayal began to sink in Janessa knew tears would shortly follow the nausea. She had to leave before anyone could question her. She was thankful her parents weren't there to learn the truth. She felt humiliated by what her grandfather had contrived, and her father would have been furious. She needed fresh air and a quiet place to think. At the moment she felt too heartsick even to pray. Her chest felt tight, and it was difficult to breathe. Somehow she needed to escape.

"Janessa, are you okay?" Rosy asked as she hurried toward the front door of the church. Her eyes had filled with tears, and she quickly wiped them away.

"I–I'll talk to you later, Rosy," she whispered, forcing the words around the lump in her throat.

When Guy's family turned to her with concerned and confused expressions Janessa ducked her head and hurried out of the church.

Now what was she to do? She was married to a man who took her as a job and not as his beloved wife.

# thirteen

Many years earlier Guy had chosen Beth Alderman as the woman to devote his heart and talent to, and Janessa had thought the world might end. Her teenage heart felt bruised beyond repair, and she didn't think she'd survive the hurt. But that pain was insignificant to the agony she felt over this betrayal. To learn someone she loved and trusted had entered her life simply for a paycheck was humiliating. She doubted she'd ever be able to face Guy again. Yet the fact that she was his legal wife made it difficult for her to avoid him.

Janessa hurried down the block and took a side street, hoping no one from the church would follow and question her before she was ready to talk. She couldn't bear the looks of pity as they learned the truth. What was evident to her now was that she couldn't please her grandfather, Guy wasn't the man she thought he was, and God must have put her through this to teach her a lesson.

If she had been smart she would have stuck with the mission her grandfather had assigned her so long ago. Work hard— it's the only way to please people—*and God*, she amended. Somewhere she had gotten distracted and now was paying the price. If she hadn't been so naive about Guy, she wouldn't be in this mess now. He was just a man, and no other man besides him had been able to distract her from her work.

"Janessa, hello!"

She looked up in surprise to find Mrs. Pembroke motioning to her from the backseat of a car parked across the street in front of a bookstore. Seeing the bookstore made her think of Guy. Now that she knew the truth would he return to his old life? She was in no mood for chitchat, but Mrs. Pembroke was a nice lady. She'd never understand if Janessa didn't stop and share a word or two with her.

Reluctantly she started to cross the street then paused. Her grandfather didn't want her near the Pembrokes. Why? She shook away the thought and crossed the rest of the way to where Mrs. Pembroke waited. The lady looked up at her expectantly, her blue hair seeming more vibrant in the afternoon sunlight.

"Janessa, get in the car with me. I want to talk to you about my painting."

*The Caravaggio.* Hadn't Ted explained the situation to her yet? Of course not, she thought, answering her own question. If Mrs. Pembroke knew the situation, maybe they could join forces and stop him from selling.

"Mrs. Pembroke, I agree we need to talk about the painting, but I have some personal issues to tend to first. May I meet with you tomorrow?"

Mrs. Pembroke shook her head emphatically. "No, no! That doesn't work at all for me. Get in the car because it's too drafty for me to get out, dear. You can't possibly know how it is for these old bones. I think we might have a storm passing through soon. I can feel it in every joint in my body."

Janessa didn't want to talk about the painting, but she also wanted to delay her return to the church where she would have to face Guy again. Deciding to handle one problem at a time, she slipped into the car next to Mrs. Pembroke. The lady's poodle yipped and wiggled in greeting but remained on Mrs. Pembroke's lap.

"You're such a good girl, Janessa. Now tell me about my painting. Where is it?"

"Where is—Ted hasn't told you, has he? He said, that is—your painting of the yellow flowers cannot be restored as—well—as we expected," Janessa faltered,. gazing at Mrs. Pembroke uncomfortably. Ted promised to explain about the forgery of the ugly yellow flowers. But he hadn't, and now it was up to her.

Mrs. Pembroke waved her bejeweled hand impatiently. "I don't care about that ugly thing, though the imitation you painted was an excellent copy. Tell me about the other, the one by Michelangelo Caravaggio. Where is it?" she demanded sharply.

Janessa stared at her incredulously. "You know about *The Maiden*? Then Ted has told you—"

"That annoying little man has told me nothing! In fact, he's caused nothing but trouble as far as I'm concerned. He even tried to convince me that forgery you painted was my real painting," Mrs. Pembroke snapped.

"Mrs. Pembroke, you really should talk to Ted Devroe about this. He's the curator and handles these situations. I'm sure you understand I don't know everything—"

"Nonsense! You know where my painting is, and I want it now. Enough games!"

Janessa stared at the agitated woman with a growing sense of dismay. Something was very wrong. When the driver turned in the front seat to glare at Janessa, she knew *everything* was wrong.

The driver was the man who had been following her, and when he spoke she recognized his voice from his threats on her answering machine and in the parking lot.

"We need to go now, Mother, before we have company." He nodded toward the back window. Janessa turned to find Guy and her grandfather hurrying down the street. Neither had spotted the car.

"Get down!" Mrs. Pembroke hissed. She grabbed Janessa by the neck and forced her head downward.

Janessa reached for the door, but Mrs. Pembroke anticipated her move. The old woman's long fingernails clawed at Janessa's arm, leaving long red scratches.

"No, you don't! This is too important. Get us out of here, Marty!"

The car sped down the street, and the faster Mrs. Pembroke's son drove, the more Janessa's spirits sank. How could she ever have guessed Mrs. Pembroke was the thief hunting for the Caravaggio?

"Where are you taking me?" Janessa asked in a flat voice. Once again she had trusted the wrong person, and this time she would probably get hurt—all because of a painting. "To the museum?"

Mrs. Pembroke shook her head, and Janessa wondered how she ever believed Mrs. Pembroke was the victim in all of this. Were her good deeds in the community a front to cover her art thievery? "Marty has been through the museum twice with no luck. But we did find the forgery—which was very good, my dear. But you can't fool an old pro. Now what did you do with the original?"

"Why don't you ask Ted since you're in this together? Isn't he the one finding a buyer for you?"

Mrs. Pembroke cackled. Her laughter filled the car, but it rang false, grating on Janessa's nerves.

"Ted Devroe? That man is straight as an arrow and would never consider selling paintings. No, this has been a difficult and carefully laid plan. I've waited years. You can't fool me with that innocent face because I know when you're lying. Now quit stalling and tell me where the painting is!"

Janessa's eyes widened when Mrs. Pembroke pulled a small

pistol from her flowered bag. The poodle growled. She had no idea if the gun was loaded or the safety on; having a real gun pointed at her set her heart racing. "I don't know where it is! Really! Please, let me go. I can't help you because I don't know anything."

Again Mrs. Pembroke cackled. This time the sound filled her with dread. "You know far *too much* for my peace of mind. Marty, take us home. Maybe a few days in the cellar will jog Janessa's memory."

*The cellar?* Janessa hoped any minute she would wake up and find this was all a nightmare. She should have taken Guy's warnings about her safety more seriously.

As Marty drove across Rochester to the old home, Mrs. Pembroke answered all Janessa's unspoken questions. Mrs. Pembroke was very proud of her plan and shared every detail. Janessa realized the more she learned, the greater trouble she was in. With all she knew it would be impossible for Mrs. Pembroke to set her free. It wouldn't matter if Mrs. Pembroke had possession of the Caravaggio again. Janessa would remain her prisoner, trapped because of her blind trust.

This second betrayal hung heavily on her shoulders. She'd trusted Mrs. Pembroke to be the person she pretended to be. What a good disguise she wore with her activities in the community, her generosity to the museum. Why, her appearance spoke of a normal little lady in her seventies with her flowing caftans and the finicky poodle she toted around. She talked about the weather and baking cookies, not stealing priceless artwork. Janessa had strived to please the woman, and she was nothing but a thief!

"My dear husband, Henry—God rest his soul—had a penchant for taking other people's property. He was very proficient at stealing valuable paintings from private collectors, and my son, Marty, has inherited his ability. One night Henry went to a party in Belgium. The man was filthy rich but so pompous. Henry didn't feel an ounce of remorse for stealing the man's painting. You call her *The Maiden*, but really she's called *Isabella*. Dear Henry had no ability for painting, but he knew what he was doing. He covered *Isabella* with those hideous yellow flowers and smuggled her out of Europe and into the United States. This was over twenty years ago, so I'm sure you don't remember the uproar. The rich Belgian was furious over his missing painting, but he never found it because my dear Henry had been so clever. Unfortunately Henry passed away before he could remove the top painting. No one else could do it. Marty has no artistic ability, and if he touched it, he would have destroyed the treasure beneath."

"So then you found me."

Mrs. Pembroke nodded enthusiastically. "I'd kept my ears open for someone just like you. I couldn't take a chance on someone older who would have heard of the scandal in Belgium. It was to my benefit that the Belgian never allowed his art collection to be documented so there were no records of *Isabella*. I had you restore several paintings to test your ability and was extremely pleased with your work. I had no doubt you would uncover *Isabella* for me and do an excellent job. Yet Ted Devroe had to stick his nose in the middle and make a mess of my business!"

"Why come after me if you suspect Ted?" Janessa asked.

Mrs. Pembroke's eyes narrowed as she studied Janessa. "He doesn't have it, does he? It would be a waste of my time to question him and raise suspicions when *you* can tell me where it's hidden."

Janessa fell silent, refusing to rise to Mrs. Pembroke's bait. True, she knew Ted didn't have the painting because her grandfather had taken it. He'd instructed Guy to put it in safekeeping somewhere, and she had no clue where that was.

With a sense of dread she realized they had arrived at Mrs. Pembroke's house. She couldn't let them force her inside. Marty seemed to anticipate her plan to run away as soon as the car door opened; he clamped his hand around her arm with a crushing hold and dragged her to the house. Janessa hoped one of Mrs. Pembroke's neighbors was nosy and would witness Marty's rough treatment of her, but the neighborhood was silent.

"Let go of me!" she screamed.

Marty clamped his hand over her mouth. "Get inside quickly," he growled, his warm breath fanning her cheek making Janessa want to vomit. What would they do to her if she couldn't reveal the painting's whereabouts?

He forced Janessa into the house and through the living room where she had enjoyed tea with Mrs. Pembroke. On several occasions they had chatted comfortably, discussing restoration techniques. Janessa had thought Mrs. Pembroke was genuinely interested in her, but it had been part of a carefully laid plan. It was obvious now—why hadn't she suspected before?

"You're such a nice girl, Janessa, that I hate to do this to you," Mrs. Pembroke murmured as she led them into the kitchen and fiddled with a lock on a small door in the far wall. "You have twenty-four hours to search your memory and tell me the location of *Isabella*. I think I'm being very generous. And if you don't tell me what I want to know, then we will see that you are put in a state mental institution. They will heavily medicate you, and no one will ever hear from you again."

Janessa suspected this was to be her fate whether she revealed the painting's location or not. As Mrs. Pembroke already said, she knew too much. "You can't do this to me! They'll know you're lying, that we're not related. You can't just admit someone to an institution." She tried to wrench her arm free from Marty's grasp, but his hold was like a steel band.

Mrs. Pembroke laughed at Janessa's effort to escape. "Ah, the kitten has claws after all! Don't worry about the details, my dear. Marty is very good at forging documents. We'll make you a new birth certificate with me listed as your mother. They'll never question anything I tell them when I show up with written proof of your mental instability. Years of therapy, doctors' reports, police reports—Marty will fix it all up."

"You won't get away with this! Someone will find me!" Janessa cried out as Marty shoved her into the cellar. She stumbled down the few stairs and landed in a heap on the dirt floor. Before she could say anything more the door slammed shut, cutting off the light that had filtered into the cellar. As the lock was forced into place, Janessa knew her chances of freedom had diminished, as well.

"Dear Lord, help me find a way out of here!" She clambered to her feet and was surprised when her head brushed the low ceiling. Frantically she searched for a switch or light fixture with a pull string. She located the electrical cord attached to the ceiling and followed it to the socket. There was no bulb.

She retraced her steps back to the staircase where a glimmer of light shone through the space under the door. After several attempts at forcing the door open, she gave up and sank down on the bottom stair.

"I have to be brave," she whispered, but she didn't feel brave anymore. She was alone with two criminals as her keepers, and no one else knew where she was. *Guy failed in the job he was hired to do,* she thought bitterly. He couldn't help her now. No one could. As her hope faded—she could never tackle this mountain alone—tears streamed unbidden down her cheeks. There was nothing she could do.

*Take courage. You are never alone. You are safe in the shadow of My wing, and I will never leave you nor forsake you.*

The words should have been a quiet comfort to Janessa's heart. Guy had told her she could trust God to take care of her, but she couldn't let go of her usual doubts. She didn't feel worthy. No matter how hard she worked and tried to please, she didn't feel as if she deserved God's favor. It was a huge part of her insecurity, she knew, and it was something she didn't like to consider. How could she please others if she couldn't please God? She worked hard because she wanted to be valued. For months her body had been telling her to back off with all the headaches, but she wouldn't listen.

*I chose you before the foundation of the world. I do not desire sacrifice; I desire to make your burden light.*

*Accept the love I have for you, through faith and not of yourself. It is my gift to you because I delight in you. My love is yours.*

Each word worked against the doubt built up in her mind. As she thought of reasons why God was angry with her, more and more scripture passages came to mind. And they weren't verses of anger and punishment. All spoke of His love and compassion for her as His Spirit ministered to her. Could God really be pleased with her? Surely He was testing her with these trials. She knew she was His child and had heard the verses about works and faith. Yet she couldn't grasp the truth.

So often, when she felt heaven was silent, she compared her heavenly Father to her earthly grandfather. When her grandfather was harsh and unyielding, she believed God was the same. When she found it impossible to please her grandfather, she expected God to turn from her in displeasure, as well. Had she been wrong?

Guy believed the Lord accepted her unconditionally, and he had tried to show her. No matter how he betrayed her, had he told her the truth about God?

"Lord," she whispered through her tears. "I'm still not sure if I can believe this. I know You loved me enough to die for my sins. I'm trying to understand that maybe You aren't angry and testing me still. I want to believe in Your unconditional love. Without work or struggle I want to receive what You have for me.

"Please help me get out of here. I'm hurt and angry by what Guy and my grandfather did. But it doesn't change how I feel. I have to tell Guy I love him. I don't understand why my grandfather made an agreement with him, but I can see how much I needed his protection. Whatever Guy's reasons, they don't change how much I love him. Please, Lord, get me out of here. I can't be separated from him forever."

Day drew into night as she waited. The only reason she knew this was because the light beneath the door began to fade. She was tired, hungry, and thirsty. She felt dirty; she was sure her beautiful, cream-colored skirt and blouse were filthy. Her wedding night wasn't supposed to be like this, and her marriage wasn't to be spent locked in an institution far away from her husband.

"I will hope in God because the joy of the Lord is my strength," Janessa murmured every time fear tried to creep back into her mind, and just the thought of God's power made her feel a little stronger.

Seconds ticked into minutes, and minutes stretched into hours as she anticipated her release. She had to trust God not to leave her to the evil devices of Mrs. Pembroke and her son. God delighted in her, and He would save her.

Janessa had grown weary from so many days of tension and exhaustion and was lying on the step when the cellar door was thrown open with a crash. She sat up, blinking at the bright light as someone rushed down the stairs toward her.

She was scooped into someone's arms, and when she smelled his familiar scent and felt his comfortable strength she knew who held her.

"I knew you'd come, Guy," she whispered as intense relief flooded through her.

Guy sat on the step, cradling Janessa close to his heart. "Ah, Nessa, I was so scared. When you disappeared from the church and everyone said how upset you were, I knew something bad had happened."

"You were right," she sniffed.

"Why did you leave?"

"I heard you talking to my grandfather. He said he hired you to take care of me, and you wanted more—more money," she faltered, finding it difficult to utter the words that had devastated her hours earlier.

"And you must have missed the part when I told your grandfather that having you as my wife was the greatest gift I could receive and that the arrangement was off. What husband wants to be paid for protecting his wife? Janessa, I never took a dime for protecting you, and from the beginning I knew I wouldn't. I agreed to help your grandfather watch over you, and somewhere along the line I fell in love. Part of me always loved you, in a different way, even when you were a teenager. But the love I feel for you now is unlike anything I've ever experienced."

"Even with Beth?" She hated asking, but she needed there to be no secrets between them.

"What I felt for Beth was nothing like this. This is love

God has orchestrated. Please don't ever compare yourself to her again. You're my wife! She has nothing to do with us." He took her hand and placed it over his heart so she could feel the steady beating. "I've changed over the past ten years, and I know my heart, Nessa. It once was broken, but today it is strong, thanks to the Lord's guiding hand. He led me to you, and I could never want anyone else."

"I love you, too," Janessa whispered. She would have said more, but Guy wouldn't allow it as his lips covered hers in a kiss that held so much promise.

As they pulled apart she asked, "I need to know something. Do you really believe God loves me unconditionally?"

"Absolutely."

"What if I sin? Or willfully choose the wrong thing? Won't I make Him angry? Don't I need to keep trying to please Him?"

"God's compassionate love is bigger than our emotions. He's not waiting to test us and condemn us. He's our loving Father who wants to guide us. He doesn't need our works. He only wants us to love Him in return."

Though it was difficult for her to grasp, she longed to believe what Guy said was true. "I have a lot of habits to break. You'll have to help me."

"God will help you because He loves you so much," he said before he kissed her again.

Soon officers requesting answers to dozens of questions interrupted them. Guy led Janessa out of the cellar into the brightly lit kitchen. As she'd feared, her clothes were ruined, but she felt like the most beautiful woman in the world.

As she was settled at the table to answer questions, her grandfather burst into the room. She wasn't surprised when he started bellowing at the police officers.

"Give us a moment of peace, will you? Can't you see my

granddaughter has gone through a traumatic experience? I want five minutes. Then you can do your job with your endless questions and mountains of paperwork."

The two officers filed out of the room, leaving Walter glowering at Janessa. She felt Guy's fingers press her shoulder in support, but she was fine. For the first time in her life she didn't bristle or feel hurt by her grandfather's look of displeasure.

"You look terrible."

"I feel wonderful," she responded.

"I'm surprised you didn't have a breakdown, stuck in that dark cellar all alone. You always hated the dark when you were little."

"But I wasn't alone. I was safe in God's arms." She could see her answer caught her grandfather off guard. He opened his mouth then promptly closed it.

"When you're ready to discuss spiritual things, Grandpa, Guy and I are here to help. God loves you, and the best part is that His love is free—that's what I'm beginning to understand. You don't have to do anything to earn it, and He loves you whether you believe it or not."

Her grandfather's glower deepened, and she was afraid he might say something rude. Instead he muttered, "I'll think about it."

When the police officers came back into the kitchen Janessa learned what had happened.

Years earlier at a different museum benefit Walter had overheard a man—Henry Pembroke—confiding how easy it was to smuggle paintings. With a cheap, ugly overlaying painting no one suspected a masterpiece was hidden beneath.

"My memory isn't so dim that I'd forget the sensation that was made over in Europe when the painting was stolen. The only detail released to the public was that it was a rare baroque period painting by Michelangelo Merisi da Caravaggio and everyone was searching for it. Very few people had the privilege of seeing *Isabella* at that time."

When Mrs. Pembroke began making contributions to the museum, Walter became suspicious. He knew what her husband had said about stealing art, and he realized Janessa could be in a vulnerable position. Not only did she restore oil paintings, but also if her talent of copying artwork ever became known, someone like Mrs. Pembroke could exploit her.

"If Ted Devroe wasn't involved, why didn't you trust him? Some of his behavior still seems suspicious to me," Janessa added.

"But he *was* involved. I confided my concerns over the Pembrokes to him. When you uncovered the Caravaggio, it confirmed what I knew we were dealing with. I told Ted to help me get the painting so we could turn it over to the authorities. He was pretty anxious to get it out of the museum. We knew the only place it would be safe from a thief like Marty Pembroke was at the police station."

Janessa shook her head, feeling perplexed by all the new information. The puzzle was coming together, but she still couldn't make out the full picture. "It seems awfully complicated. You should have told me this rather than going behind my back. All the time I suspected Ted, and you knew it was Mrs. Pembroke."

A pained expression crossed Walter's face. "By that time you were heavily involved, and my biggest concern was keeping you safe. I thought if either you or Guy knew of my suspicions you might act differently around Mrs. Pembroke. We couldn't let you tip her off since the police were so close to solving the crime. They encouraged me to tell you nothing, but I had to make sure you were safe. I couldn't trust Ted Devroe to do it because he didn't love you—he exploits you in his own way. I was so afraid you would agree to marry him; he's made comments to me about his intentions for the last year. He may be an upstanding man in his church, but he's too critical. You'd be miserable with him, and I wasn't certain he'd keep you safe. So I turned to Guy. He's always treated you right, and I knew I could trust him."

One thing still didn't make sense to Janessa. "How did you find me in the cellar?"

This time Guy spoke up. "Walter knew the Pembrokes wanted the painting, and when you disappeared from the church he suspected they had kidnapped you. The Pembrokes have been following us, waiting for the chance to get you alone. Walter set up a trade—you for the priceless masterpiece."

Janessa stared at her grandfather in surprise. "You gave them the painting?"

Walter smiled. "Of course not! The police released the painting to me but didn't let me out of their sight. When I handed the painting to Mrs. Pembroke and Marty, the police were there to arrest them immediately. While that was happening, Guy was already on his way over here to find you. He was so frantic I nearly begged the police to arrest him instead. If he had come for you too soon, it might have ruined everything. But now you are safe, the painting has been recovered, and the Belgian family will be notified in the next few days."

Janessa turned in her seat to stare at her wonderful husband. "You knew I was here the entire time?"

He nodded. "I prayed for you every minute and suffered with not knowing what was happening to you." He bent down and pressed a firm kiss to her lips.

She rested her hand against his cheek. "I was safe."

"God kept you safe," he affirmed.

Walter cleared his throat, and both Guy and Janessa turned to look at him. A deep flush had risen to his cheeks, and he looked uncomfortable.

"Grandpa, are you okay?"

He cleared his throat again. "I know I'm just a stubborn old man, and I have a few fences to mend with you."

"What are you trying to say?"

"I wanted you to take after me. But you didn't, and it made me mad. I'm not angry anymore even though I probably sound like it. . . . I guess what I'm trying to tell you is I'm proud of you."

Tears filled Janessa's eyes, and she reached to give her grandfather a hug. Rather than patting her back awkwardly as he had in the past, he clung to her, robbing her of breath.

When Walter released her, Guy took her back in his arms. Everything seemed to fade away as she gazed into his eyes. "Don't we have a honeymoon to plan, Mrs. Langly?" he murmured for her ears only.

Janessa's heart leaped, and she knew all the good things in her life were because of God. She had the husband she'd always loved, and her relationship with her grandfather was on new ground. Most importantly, she was seeing how God's love was free for everyone to receive.

There were no words to express all that was in her heart, so she boldly pressed her lips to her husband's, then whispered, "I believe we do, Mr. Langly."

# A Letter To Our Readers

Dear Reader:

In order that we might better contribute to your reading enjoyment, we would appreciate your taking a few minutes to respond to the following questions. We welcome your comments and read each form and letter we receive. When completed, please return to the following:

Fiction Editor
Heartsong Presents
PO Box 719
Uhrichsville, Ohio 44683

1. Did you enjoy reading *Safe In His Arms* by Tish Davis?
   ❏ Very much! I would like to see more books by this author!
   ❏ Moderately. I would have enjoyed it more if

   _____

   _____

   _____

2. Are you a member of **Heartsong Presents**? ❏ Yes ❏ No
   If no, where did you purchase this book? _____

   _____

3. How would you rate, on a scale from 1 (poor) to 5 (superior), the cover design? _____

4. On a scale from 1 (poor) to 10 (superior), please rate the following elements.

   ____ Heroine          ____ Plot
   ____ Hero             ____ Inspirational theme
   ____ Setting          ____ Secondary characters

5. These characters were special because? _____
_____
_____

6. How has this book inspired your life? _____
_____
_____

7. What settings would you like to see covered in future
**Heartsong Presents** books? _____
_____
_____

8. What are some inspirational themes you would like to see
treated in future books? _____
_____
_____

9. Would you be interested in reading other **Heartsong
Presents** titles? ❏ Yes   ❏ No

10.  Please check your age range:
   ❏ Under 18          ❏ 18-24
   ❏ 25-34             ❏ 35-45
   ❏ 46-55             ❏ Over 55

Name_____
Occupation _____
Address _____
City, State, Zip_____

# Colorado
# WEDDINGS

## 3 stories in 1

Enjoy the ride as three determined men attempt to convince three stubborn career women to take the walk down the aisle to love's surprising treasures.

Titles by author Joyce Livingston include: *A Winning Match*, *Downhill*, and *The Wedding Planner*.

Contemporary, paperback, 352 pages, 5³⁄₁₆" x 8"

---

Please send me ____ copies of *Colorado Weddings*. I am enclosing $6.97 for each. (Please add $3.00 to cover postage and handling per order. OH add 7% tax. If outside the U.S. please call 740-922-7280 for shipping charges.)

Name_____

Address _____

City, State, Zip _____

To place a credit card order, call 1-740-922-7280.
Send to: Heartsong Presents Readers' Service, PO Box 721, Uhrichsville, OH 44683

# Presents

HEARTSONG

PRESENTS

# If you love Christian romance…

$10.<sup>99</sup>

You'll love Heartsong Presents' inspiring and faith-filled romances by today's very best Christian authors. . .DiAnn Mills, Wanda E. Brunstetter, and Yvonne Lehman, to mention a few!

When you join Heartsong Presents, you'll enjoy four brand-new, mass market, 176-page books—two contemporary and two historical—that will build you up in your faith when you discover God's role in every relationship you read about!

Mass Market 176 Pages

Imagine. . .four new romances every four weeks—with men and women like you who long to meet the one God has chosen as the love of their lives…all for the low price of $10.99 postpaid.

To join, simply visit www.heartsong presents.com or complete the coupon below and mail it to the address provided.

## YES! Sign me up for Heartsng!

**NEW MEMBERSHIPS WILL BE SHIPPED IMMEDIATELY!**
**Send no money now.** We'll bill you only $10.99 postpaid with your first shipment of four books. Or for faster action, call 1-740-922-7280.

NAME _____

ADDRESS_____

CITY_____ STATE _____ ZIP _____

MAIL TO: HEARTSONG PRESENTS, P.O. Box 721, Uhrichsville, Ohio 44683
or sign up at **WWW.HEARTSONGPRESENTS.COM**